BUILD
UNIVERSES

Sean Joseph White

Châtelaillon-Plage

© 2020 **Europe Books**
europe-books.co.uk

ISBN 979-12-201-0080-9
First edition: July 2020

Châtelaillon-Plage

I

The Dorchester Hotel

Stephen Fry, the actor and polymath, took to the stage to great applause. He stepped up to the podium and, with his usual self-deprecation, silenced the crowd with humble gratitude.

"The Trinity prize for art is awarded each year to the amateur artist, in the United Kingdom, who, in the eyes of the judging panel, has produced the most professional work of art in the previous year.

2017 has been an outstanding year for amateur art in the UK and there are five nominees for the Blue Riband. The winner will receive £50,000.00 and their artwork will be exhibited at the Royal Academy.

The nominees are:

Dickson Smith for "Sentinel". A statue in bronze. Britannia dressed as one of "The Few".

Blair MacLeod for "The Minch". Oil on canvas. Painting of a fishing boat being tossed in a storm at sea.

Theresa Agumanu for "Mudda". Carved wooden statue. Mother as Buddha.

Sylvia Starrs for "Aurora Borealis". Colour photograph. The Northern Lights over Scotland.

Gilbert Martin for "Châtelaillon-Plage". Oil on canvas. Painting of a recurring dream.

And the winner is. Drum roll if you please".

Stephen smiled at the audience as he struggled to open the gold envelope. He eventually managed to pull the white card from its prison. He read it, smiled, and put his mouth to the microphone.

"Gilbert Martin for "Châtelaillon-Plage."

The cheers were deafening. The other contestants rose out of their seats to give a standing ovation. Gilbert Martin, in shock, was pushed out of his seat by his literary agent, Eleanor Macdonald. She pointed to the stage and mouthed "get up there".

Gilbert started walking towards the stage in a daze. Two assistants walked out with a large easel and placed his painting on the stand for the press to take photographs. There was a flurry of flashes as the photographers closed in on the picture.

The painting was a beach scene, in the late afternoon. It depicted a young girl of about 13 handing a little boy of the same age, an ice cream. The colours were dazzling. Sky blue, pale yellow, Naples yellow, French ochre, yellow ochre, ultra-marine and turquoise.

He climbed the steps and shook hands with Stephen, "Well done, Gilbert. It is outstanding."

He nodded and stepped up to the podium. 'I would like to thank Margaux Martin, whoever and wherever she is.

Thank you for the ice cream. Thank you for the French kiss.

I'm sorry that my letter may not have lived up to expectations or, if you did not receive it, then I curse fate and will just have to remain disappointed forever.

Wherever you are, I hope that life has been kind to you and, you never know, perhaps, one day we will meet again, in the twilight, on Châtelaillon-Plage. Thank you."

As he left the stage, he caught a glimpse of Eleanor. She had removed the handkerchief from her sleeve and was drying her eyes. His agent was the only person who knew the whole story. He had, after all, written a book about it.

As he got to the bottom of the steps, he was stopped by a BBC reporter who was brandishing a microphone, "Mr Martin, if you could give us one minute."

He smiled and nodded. He recognised the reporter. She normally did politics on the news.

"First of all, congratulations. You must feel very proud."

Gilbert nodded, "It's nice to be acknowledged for something that you have invested an awful lot of time in. I have been painting now for about five years and in that time, I've calculated that I have spent over four thousand hours painting in oils.

This has all been done in between writing my books. It hasn't been easy because I'm not a natural. I view the prize as an acknowledgement of all the serious hard work that has gone in to it."

The reporter eagerly nodded her head in the way that reporters do when they are live on television, "The painting is wonderful, if you don't mind me saying, and there obviously appears to be a story attached to it, can you enlighten us?"

Gilbert smiled, "Firstly, thank you for being kind. The painting is a story and is actually the subject of my next novel, so I don't want to give away too much at this time. If you attend the launch of the book, I'll let you have the first question.

I'll say only this. The painting is my way of coming to terms with what might have been. It is the story of a broken heart."

She looked delighted, "I'll hold you to that promise of the first question. Gilbert Martin, Thank you very much and congratulations again."

He pressed his way through the milling photographers and made his way back to his seat. Eleanor hugged him and whispered in his ear, "That was excellent. You've set up everything nicely for the book launch. I can feel the intrigue."

He chuckled, "Trust you to worry about the launch. I think the story is a very good one and I genuinely don't want to spoil it for people. I think they will love the story."

She squeezed him tighter, "Oh, Gilbert. It is a wonderful work. I think you are going to win every award going. Nobel prize, if you ask me."

He looked up at the ceiling, "It's not even in the shops yet. Listen, Eleanor. If you go overboard on this, you run the risk of spoiling something that is very important to me. Please don't ruin it."

She put her hands on his shoulders, "I won't ruin it for you, Gilbert. I want you to be happy, more than anything else."

He sat down and closed his eyes for a moment. The noise was almost unbearable. It was at moments like this, more than any other, that he welcomed a visit. There was a flash of the usual white light and she was there at his side, "Don't worry. It won't last long. You'll be home soon."

He moved his hand to touch her, but someone shouted out behind him and he opened his eyes. She was gone.

Eleanor said goodbye to him on the steps of the Dorchester Hotel, "We are going for launch on Friday, so enjoy the next few days. I will be in my office. If you need me for anything, let me know. Until then, fingers crossed."

He kissed her goodbye and hailed a taxi.

"Phillimore Gardens, Kensington, please." Gilbert could see the driver quietly curse. He sympathised. He was only 10 minutes from The Dorchester and the driver was probably expecting a better fair.

He sat in the back seat and watched Park Lane drift by as they headed for Marble Arch. It gave him time to reflect on the evening's events.

He wasn't surprised he had won. He had honed his skills over the years to the point where he could paint a very decent portrait within four hours. Châtelaillon-Plage had taken him seven months. He had spent a lot of that time with his eyes closed, replaying the memory over and over again. The perfect day.

"Are you English, Monsieur?"

He smiled. He had loved being called Monsieur, "No. I'm Scottish, actually. I'm from Edinburgh."

She had raised her eyebrows, "Scotland. It is where the monster lives."

He had laughed as he had wiped the sweat from his brow, "Yes, she lives in the loch."

She looked concerned, "You are hot, Monsieur. I will buy you an ice cream if you tell me about this loch."

They had walked arm in arm to the ice cream vendor, "What would you like?"

He had replied in French, "Je voudrais une glace malaga, s'il vous plâit, Madame."

She had laughed and bought him a rum and raisin ice cream and a vanilla one for herself.

"Now tell me about this loch." Her hand had reached out to hand him the cornet.

The sound of a voice interrupted his thoughts, "That will be £6.40, please mate."

He shook himself awake and went in to his coat pocket for his wallet. He pulled out a ten-pound note, "Many thanks and keep the change."

He got out of the car and walked up to the front door of the house and pulled out his key. He opened the door, switched on the hall light, and locked the front door behind him.

"Home at last," she said.

"Yes, home at last. Will I make us toast and tea?"

She chuckled, "You make it and tell me about the loch again."

He shrugged, "If you like." He went through in to the kitchen and put on the kettle. He extracted two slices of bread from the bread-bin and placed them in the toaster.

"Loch Ness is one of the largest lochs in Scotland. It holds the most water. It is the second longest and it is the deepest by average depth. It is the perfect home for the monster.

Scientists believe that the creature may be a left over from the age of the dinosaurs with some thinking that it may be an Elasmosaurus or a Plesiosaur.

I think that this is a bit of a fancy. It is probably a newer creature which remains, as yet, undiscovered and unclassified."

"Do you think we will ever see it?" she asked.

He held up his hand, "Who knows, mon amour. Who knows."

It was very late, and his hand hovered over the button on the CD player, "Is it too late, do you think?"

She hesitated, "Oh, play it but just the once and then we can go to bed."

He pressed play. The both sang along.

Just a perfect day
Eat ice cream cones on the sand
And then later
I hold your hand, then go home

Just a perfect day
Feed animals just like you (They pointed at each other)
Then later
A kiss or two, and then home

Oh, it's such a perfect day
I'm glad I spent it with you
Oh, such a perfect day
You just keep me hanging on
You just keep me hanging on

Just a perfect day
Problems all left alone
Weekenders on our own
It's such fun

Just a perfect day
You made me forget myself
I thought I was
Someone else, someone good
Oh, it's such a perfect day
I'm glad I spent it with you
Oh, …

The kettle boiled, and he heard the toaster pop. He made his tea and buttered his toast.

She put her hand on his shoulder, "Are you going to see that woman tomorrow?"

He bit in to his toast, "I have to. I need a cover story. People know that I take medication. If they see me talking to someone who isn't there, they just give me the loony look and walk away, you do want to be free, I assume?"

She laughed, "More than anything. You are very clever; do you know that? I knew it the minute I saw you. The minute you walked on to my beach."

"It is your beach now? When did it become your beach?"

She laughed again, "Okay, it is our beach, but you, Monsieur. You belong to me."

He turned around, "I have always been yours, Madame, and I will be yours forever. Never worry about that. There is not one minute of every day when I do not think about you. We were meant to be together and we will be together. Always."

She put her hands on his cheeks, "I know, Monsieur. I cannot leave you now. You are like a strong magnet. There is nowhere for me to go."

Gilbert frowned, "What do you mean by strong magnet. You don't think I'm forcing you to be here, do you?"

She giggled, "Not forcing in a bad way but it is like the moth and the candle flame. I am magically drawn to you and I cannot easily fly away."

II

The Dream

The following morning, Gilbert found himself in the Harley Street waiting room of Dr Savannah Wilde, psychiatrist to those who found themselves in the public eye. Gilbert had been introduced to her by his agent at some party two years earlier. He knew it hadn't been an accident.

"Gilbert, she knows what she's doing. You are very vulnerable to gossip and she can take all of that away. She is, on the one hand, discrete, but on the other, she'll get in touch with the right people and make sure you are handled with the right care. Her husband is an attorney. Trust me, it works."

Gilbert smiled. She had been correct. It did work.

He looked around at the wood panelled room. He liked it here. It somehow reminded him of Edwardian England. Brandy and cigars. Men dressed in dinner jackets and black ties.

"Mrs Wilde will see you now, Mr Martin." The receptionist held the door open for him and he walked through to his appointment.

"Ah, Gilbert, I believe congratulations are in order." She got up from behind her desk and ushered him on to the oxblood leather Cambridge couch. She was wearing a dress patterned with flowers and he could detect the smell of Baccarat perfume. Expensive.

"When I saw the painting, I nearly fainted. I take it that I know the subjects?"

Gilbert sat back on the couch, "Yes, of course you do. The painting depicts the moment when Margaux hands me the ice cream, it is indelibly imprinted on my memory."

She laughed, "I'll say! How long ago was it exactly"?

Gilbert thought for a moment, "It will be 35 years exactly, this June. The 29th to be precise."

She whistled, "Wow! And you've dreamt about that day, every night for 35 years?"

He nodded, "Yes. Every night, without fail. I am neither permitted, nor would I permit myself to forget it."

She looked at him curiously, "And why is that?"

He looked down at the floor, "That's what I'm hoping to find out. It is the reason I've written my book.

I know you are treating me as a patient and I have no problem with that, however, to me, this is not an illness. This is a mystery. I need to know why Margaux followed me off that beach, that day, and why she came home with me to Scotland.

Don't get me wrong. I've never regarded the meeting with Margaux as just some accident and I've never, ever, seen her as just another person that I bumped in to. Something mysterious happened and with the help of my book, I feel I have a chance of finding out."

Dr Wilde put her notes down on the coffee table, "Gilbert, I want you to know that I also view this as a mystery and I can assure you, I am greatly intrigued.

From a medical perspective, I am seeing this as an opportunity for a catharsis. If you do find out something, then hopefully, it will help you put all of this to bed.

However, I think it would be wise and helpful if you kept me updated as to what is going on. I'm giving you my mobile phone number so that you can keep in touch.

When are you going to France?"

Gilbert sighed, "I'm not sure. I want to see how things

go first. The book launches on Friday and I'm hoping to go over shortly after that.

The painting was a means to an end. It was to get people interested in the story and when they read the book, hopefully they will respond positively. My one worry is that I'll be seen as a lunatic and be disparaged in the press. If that happens then I think it would spoil all my plans."

Dr Wilde leaned forward, "Let me assure you, Gilbert, that will not happen. I have friends who are ready and willing to jump to your defence at a moment's notice. There will be no disparagement."

Gilbert relaxed. The purpose of this meeting had been achieved. He merely nodded his thanks.

"Now, how are you getting on with your medication?"

He shrugged, "It is doing what it is supposed to do, I guess. I am not suffering from any depression at the moment and there have been no manic episodes. I guess I'm feeling as cool as a cucumber."

She paused for a moment, "And the dream? Are you still having it with the medication?"

Gilbert chuckled, "There is no amount of narcotic that can stop that from happening. I have it every night and it is always exactly the same.

She pursed her lips, "Go over it one more time for me, just so that I have it fresh in my memory before you go off to France."

He laughed, "With pleasure. I never tire of it.

I arrive on the beach by coach from La Rochelle, where the school has booked out a hotel for a week.

There are about twenty of us and everybody disappears in their little groups. I detach myself from my three friends and say that I want to walk along the shoreline. They are pre-occupied by some French pornography that they've managed to acquire.

I take off my socks and shoes and put them in my rucksack. I start walking along the beach and I let the waves rush over my bare feet. Suddenly, in the white light of the sun, I hear a voice. It is a girl about my age.

"Bonjour" she says.

"Oh, hello."

"Are you English, Monsieur?"

I remember smiling, "No. I'm Scottish, actually. I'm from Edinburgh."

She raises her eyebrows, "Scotland. It is where the monster lives."

I laugh and then wipe the sweat from my brow, "Yes, she lives in the loch."

She looks concerned, "You are hot, Monsieur. I will buy you an ice cream if you tell me about this loch."

We walk arm in arm to the ice cream van, "What would you like?"

I give her my best French, "Je voudrais une glace malaga, s'il vous plait, Madame."

She laughs and buys me a rum and raisin ice cream and a vanilla one for herself.

"Now tell me about this loch."

"Loch Ness is one of the largest lochs in Scotland. It holds the most water. It is the second longest and it is the deepest by average depth. It is the perfect home for the monster.

Scientists believe that the creature may be a left over from the age of the dinosaurs with some thinking that it may be an Elasmosaurus or a Plesiosaur."

She is very interested, "I think I would like to see this loch and the monster."

I lick my ice cream, "Maybe you could come back to Scotland with me and we could go and have a look."

She smiles, "I think I would like that very much."

We sit down on the beach together and she draws out a

map on the wet sand, "This is France, and this is Scotland. Where is the loch on the map?"

I take my index finger and make a hole in the sand where Inverness is, "Right there!"

She leans forward and kisses me on the lips. I kiss her back.

She holds out her hand, "Come on. Let's take a walk."

We hold hands, all the way along Châtelaillon-Plage. At the end of the beach there are rocky pools. We sit down and take a look, "I think Loch Ness is bigger than this" she says laughing.

I laugh too, "Just a bit."

"My name is Margaux Martin. What's yours?"

I look stunned, "My name is Gilbert Martin. We are both the same."

She smiles and looks pleased, "Obviously. I think we are married. Do you want to kiss the bride?"

I lean forward and open my mouth just a bit. She grabs my cheeks and kisses me full on. Her tongue brushes against mine. It is electric.

There is a voice in the distance, "Margaux. Margaux."

She looks at me, "Maman. I must go, for now. I will see you again, Gilbert Martin."

She gets up and walks toward the road. She climbs up the sand and just before she leaves, she looks back and waves. I wave back. She's gone."

Dr Wilde sat in her seat without moving for several minutes. When she eventually spoke, her voice was shaking, "It is a great story, Gilbert. I predict that you will have no problems with disparagement. You would have to be a heartless stone not to respond to that story at some emotional level."

He was happy. He hated anyone making light of his situation. It was too important to him.

"I think I would like to leave you on the medication you

are on for just now and we'll monitor things. My preference would be for you to sleep without dreams but as you say, the likelihood of that happening before you have a resolution to the situation is zero."

She wrote out another prescription for him and handed it over, "Enjoy your trip to France and please, please, keep in touch."

He pocketed the little piece of white paper and promised that he would.

When he got outside, he looked up at the sky. It was a beautiful day and he decided to walk home. If he skirted Hyde Park, it would take him an hour. If he went through the park, he might dally, and it would take him an hour and a half. He decided he would go through the park.

It was a quiet day for visitors. He entered the park at Bayswater Road and stopped to have a look at the Italian Water Gardens. He understood that the gardens had been a gift from Prince Albert to Queen Victoria. In his mind's eye, he hoped this was true. It would have been a lovely thing to have done. He could imagine the delight on the Queen's face when the gift was revealed.

He thought about his own queen and when he did, he went back, as he always did, to the 29th June 1983 on Châtelaillon-Plage. He remembered as he was about to get on the coach at the end of the afternoon. She had rushed up to him and pressed a little envelope in to his hand, "It is a letter with my address on it. Write to me."

She kissed him on the cheek and rushed away. He anxiously looked for her over the heads of all the people. She disappeared over the sand and on to the road. He was sure she looked back, one last time.

When he got on the bus he had sat next to one of the girls, Swotty Watts, the insufferable know it all. She had asked him if he was in love. He had told her to shut her face.

He chuckled at the thought.

It was later that evening, when he was in the bathroom brushing his teeth that she put in her first appearance, "What are you doing here?"

She had just smiled, "I'm coming home with you. We are going to see the monster, remember?"

He hadn't thought anything odd or peculiar about it. He had assumed it was a very pleasant dream. It turned out to be a wonderful dream that would last all of his life.

He turned away from the fountains and walked the rest of the way through the park. When he got to the end of Phillimore Gardens, his anticipation increased. He knew that she would be waiting for him.

He put the key in the door and let himself in.

"What did she say?"

He felt elated, "She said that if anyone poked fun at me, she would arrange to take them to court. I am pretty sure that in a couple of weeks, we will be completely free."

"Le jour de gloire est arrivé."

III

Margaux

He took his coat off and went through in to the kitchen. He clicked on the kettle and sat down at the breakfast bar.

"I had to recount my dream to her again, from the very beginning. I stopped when you handed me the letter and I got on the coach. I didn't say anything about you turning up in the hotel bathroom later."

She laughed, "Probably very wise, for now."

He propped his elbow up against the breakfast bar and leaned his chin against his hand, "Do you remember what happened after you said goodbye to me?"

She looked up at the ceiling, "I've told you before, I remember nothing until I saw you at the hotel. I remember waving to you and then it's a blank after that. The next thing I know, I was standing behind you and you were brushing your teeth. It is a mystery to me too."

He nodded, "I think that is the mystery I would like to solve. What happened to you and why did you pick me?"

She sat beside him, "I don't think that is a mystery. We are married. Where else would I be but with my husband?"

He chuckled, "I love it when you say that word. Husband. Do you think we are really married?"

She nodded, "Of course. What do you think happened before there were priests? You don't have to go to a church to be married. You kissed the bride. Don't you remember?"

He closed his eyes, "Of course, I remember. I think about

it every day."

She was pleased, "Well. There you go, then."

The kettle boiled, and he poured himself a cup of coffee, "There has been something troubling me."

She put on a tired face, "Not again. Out with it."

He sighed, "What happens when I go to France? Are you coming with me or do you think you should stay here?"

She thought about it, "I'd better stay here but will come if you call me, as always. Don't be afraid. I'll be here when you get back. I will never leave you."

He sipped his coffee, "What if I find out something dreadful?"

She looked earnestly in to his eyes, "What are you afraid of?"

He hesitated before answering, "What if something terrible happened to you? What if that was the reason you decided to come home with me? What if you don't remember anything because it is just too horrific to remember, and you simply put it out of your mind?"

She shushed him, "What if, what if, what if. What if I fell in love with you and couldn't live without you? What if I had been waiting for you all my life? It doesn't matter. We are here now, and we are happy. You do love me, do you not?"

He frowned, "I don't know how you can ask that question? I have given up everything for you. Not that I mind. I don't think I could have been happier."

She looked at him pleadingly, "Then don't worry. Whatever happens, it will all turn out all right."

He relaxed a little, "Do you know what day Thursday is?"

She pretended not to know, "I have no idea."

There was a little smile playing about her lips which informed Gilbert that she knew very well what day Thursday was.

"It is our birthday."

She feigned surprise, "Is it? Well, it is actually your birthday. We have no idea when my birthday is."

He snuggled up to her, "It is our birthday. I don't want a birthday if it is not your birthday too."

"Okay, it is our birthday. Are you going to buy a cake?"

He laughed, "Of course, I'm buying a cake. I'm going to buy a rum baba and serve it with une sauce malaga."

She put her hand to her mouth, "It will be like your ice cream that I bought for you on Châtelaillon-Plage."

"Yes, darling. It will be like our ice cream."

"How old will we be?"

He picked her up and put her on his lap, "We will be 48 years old assuming that you too were born in 1970."

She thought about it, "Yes, I'm pretty sure I was born in 1970."

Gilbert decided it was time to have another attempt at dredging as much information from her as he could. He was leaving to go to France in the next week and the more she could tell him, the better the outcome would be.

"Tell me everything that you remember about yourself. I know it's all a bit sketchy but the more you can tell me, however small, the better it will be."

She shrugged, "I think you know it all by now but if you insist. I think I was born in the town that I was named after. Margaux. It is famous for the wine.

We had a house on the Avenue Jeanne d'Arc. It was what you would call a bungalow.

My father had a brown car called a Citroen DS. I remember that very well. Everybody liked it.

I remember the day I met you and from that point on, every other memory seemed to slip away. I'm sorry but I just can't bring it back. I've tried to remember what Maman looked like and I just can't. It is gone."

He hugged her tightly, "Don't worry. I think that will be

enough. The fact that you can remember the street is good. I think that is going to help enormously."

She nodded, "Tell me where we are with your plan and what you are going to do next?"

Gilbert took another sip of his coffee, "Phase one is complete. I have painted the picture and entered it into the Trinity prize. The fact that it won is just an added bonus.

Eleanor and Savannah have been prepared for the launch of the book, so they are both completely aware of what is going on. Eleanor knows the whole story and Savannah knows the story but thinks there is a medical root cause. She believes that I am mentally ill and that I'm actually taking her medication, which of course, I'm not.

I have put the idea in the minds of the press reporters and I now expect a big presence at the book launch. When I launch the book, I will give them more of the tale in an effort to secure help on social media to trace your whereabouts in France at the time you came home with me.

Phase two is to go to France and find out what happened to you. I am going on French TV to do an interview and my expectation is that I will get a lot of direct feedback at that time. I am not looking forward to the press intrusion, but it will, hopefully, be a means to an end.

Phase three is to use the information we find out in France to free us both from this existence of hiding away all the time. If I can convince everyone that there is a medical issue then they won't think twice about me speaking to someone who is, as far as they are concerned, not there.

If I can come up with a better solution, then I will but, I need to find out what happened first. That is the plan as things stand."

She smiled, "It is a brilliant plan. I am already excited. I feel that it has a very good chance of working."

Gilbert was happy that she was happy, "Yes, I am excited

too. This is our one and only chance to bring you out in to the open, as it were. It is also my opportunity to prove to people that I am not the lunatic they think I am."

She turned around and looked at him with a concerned expression, "Does it bother you, having people who think you are mad."

He knew he was on rocky ground, "Not really but I'd prefer it if they thought about it differently. Instead of saying "that man is mad", they might say instead "there goes a man with skills that we don't have. He has supernatural powers."

She laughed out loud, "Are you trying to get everyone to believe that you are a super hero?"

It was his turn to laugh, "Yes. Madame. That is exactly what I am trying to do. I have thought for some time now that I am hyper sensitive to some things. It is not just you. I can, for instance, smell danger before it comes my way. I sometimes get a very odd feeling that something is going to happen.

Don't forget what happened at last year's Grand National. I knew with three days to go that One for Arthur was going to win and he did. We won £1500.00, remember?"

She raised her eyebrows, "Yes, that is true. I still haven't worked out how you knew it was going to win."

He kissed her cheek, "Super powers. That's how."

She snuggled in to him, "I see that you have been ordering wine on the internet. I take it, this is for our birthday?"

"Yes. I have invited Eleanor, her partner, Dr Wilde, and her husband to dinner next Saturday. I am doing a three-course meal, which I think you'll like and I'm serving Chateau Margaux for the main course. I've bought several bottles of the 1983 to commemorate the year we met. It is a vintage year, so they will probably love it.

I have also bought a bottle of the 1970 to commemorate the year we were born. It is not a classic year but I'm sure it will taste good just the same. I thought we would keep that one for ourselves and drink it when they had gone." He looked at her face to see if she was happy. Her little smile told him that she was.

"How much were the bottles?"

He shrugged, "I managed to get the 1983 for £450.00 per bottle and the 1970 was £182.00. I think we did quite well."

She was falling asleep in his arms, "I'll take your word for it, Monsieur. I think I would like to go to bed now."

"Of course, my darling." He lifted her up in his arms and carried her through to the bedroom. He pulled back the duvet and laid her head on the pillow and tucked her in, "Sleep well, my love."

Gilbert returned to the kitchen to finish his coffee. He was sure that his plan was going to work. He had meticulously engineered everything, and he considered the hard part done. The painting, which was now hanging at The Royal Academy. He wondered if it would be a good idea to drop by and have a look at it. It could mean more good publicity.

The more he thought about it, the more he liked the idea. He would drop by tomorrow to get the lie of the land and then he would decide what to do. He could always phone Eleanor and get her to contact someone who could write an article about it or better still a small piece for television.

He drank the last dregs of his cup of coffee. He would think about the whole thing overnight and decide in the morning. As he was about to go to bed, he noticed a large envelope addressed to him on the kitchen bunker. Margaux must have picked it up and put it there after the mail had been delivered.

It was his mother's handwriting. He had phoned her about a week ago and asked her to send down all his documentation from Edinburgh. He was going to need his passport to get to France.

He left the large envelope unopened. He would see to everything in the morning. It was time to go to bed. He turned out the light.

IV

The Royal Academy

The alarm went off at 7.00. There was something about a Tuesday morning that had always made him want to stay in bed. He thought it might have something to do with the fact that the working week wasn't even halfway through. As he did not need to work, he didn't need to get out of bed. He turned over and slept on until 8.00.

When he woke up, he lifted his mobile phone from the bedside table and phoned Eleanor, "I'm going in to the Royal Academy this morning to view the painting. I thought it might be a good idea if someone from the press could be there."

She sounded excited, "I think I can do better than that. Remember the BBC reporter, you said could have the first question at the launch. She has been in touch, wanting to do a piece on the painting. I'll phone her now and see if she can get a camera to Burlington House."

He got up and showered and then he changed in to moleskin trousers and stout walking shoes. He was going to walk to the Royal Academy and that meant going through Hyde Park to Buckingham Palace and then on to Piccadilly.

He went through in to the kitchen, put the kettle on and put two slices of toast in to the toaster. He opened the cupboard door and reached in for the marmalade.

"I see you are having the good stuff this morning!"

Gilbert chuckled, "When I eat it, I think of you."

The month after they had come home from France in

1983, they had visited Loch Ness with Gilbert's mother. On the way, they had stopped at one of those luxury food halls which are so popular in the Scottish Highlands. They had bought a jar of McKay's Dundee Orange Marmalade and had eaten it ever since. They had come to the conclusion that it was one of the best.

He buttered his toast and pulled a generous helping of the marmalade with a teaspoon.

He concentrated, "I like the way you have to sort of tease it from the spoon. It's a bit like getting ketchup from the bottle."

She laughed, "I love your loyalty to exquisite products."

He nodded, "Never forget the golden rule of time, manner, place. These are the signposts which deliver the greatest produce on the earth.

Think of the wines of your home. Time, first of all. They take the time. The product is not made or consumed until the time is right. If it takes twenty years, then it takes twenty years.

Manner. Only the best grapes are used and then only the best in combination to complement each other. Why? Anything else would be a waste. Mistakes cannot be made. The soil is too rich, the weather, too perfect, the knowledge of the French artisan, too unique. If you have to send a hunchback to the mouth of the Gironde estuary, to sniff the air, to tell you what type of vintage it is going to be, then that is what you do.

Place. The grapes are grown on terraces which make the best of the sun and the soil. Where the hedgerows drip the scent of herbs, ancient yellow stone, black fruits, and the memories of the great vintages. Places which are named appropriately for such a magnificent product. Latour, St Julien, Chateau Lafite, Petrus and, of course, the greatest beauty of them all, Margaux! Exquisite products, my love, should be treated with the respect they deserve."

She sat staring at him, "I love you, Monsieur. With all of my heart."

He smiled, "Thank you. I love you too."

He sat at the breakfast bar to eat his toast and drink his coffee.

"Why have you put your walking shoes on?"

He sipped his drink, "I'm walking to Burlington House to view our painting. I wondered if you would like to come with me?"

Her eyes lit up, "Truly? I would be delighted, Monsieur."

They set off at 10.00 and it wasn't long before they were in the park. Gilbert thought it best to avoid other people on the grounds that it would allow Margaux to ask questions if she needed to. As they passed Buckingham Palace, she did just that.

"Do you think Her Majesty keeps a fine cellar in the palace?"

Gilbert thought about it for a moment, "I bet she does, for personal use, and I bet it's full of absolute crackers. When it comes to the state banquets and such like, Her Majesty will order in enough of one vintage for the guests, but I wouldn't be surprised if there were a few historical belters in the personal stock."

"Speculate for me, Monsieur?"

Gilbert chuckled, "Let's see. If it were me, then I'd have kept back some of the following vintage years for Bordeaux. So, any of the premier crus from 1900, 1928/29, 1945, 1947 and 1959. I hear that our Chateau Margaux Premier Grand Cru Classé 1929 is one of the best ever. I've been trying to buy a bottle of it but have not been lucky. I might try and get a bottle when I'm in France."

Her expression changed, and Gilbert knew that she had come to a decision, "When you are down in Bordeaux, I order you to find some of the very best. We will celebrate upon your return."

Gilbert nodded. The more he thought about it, the more he liked the idea.

They walked along Piccadilly until he could see Fortnum & Mason in the distance, "We'll buy our lunch in there, when we are finished in the Royal Academy."

She smiled her agreement but pointed her finger at Burlington House, "Venice in London, Monsieur."

She wasn't kidding. The street façade of the Royal Academy was Palladian in style and definitely reminded him of 16th century Venice. It was magnificent. They entered the complex by the archway. Almost immediately, he bumped in to Eleanor.

"Good news. The BBC want to do a piece on the painting. They'll be here at 11.30."

Gilbert was chuffed, "Excellent. I think I'm going to give a few more details away on the story and talk a little bit more about my mental health. Not the whole thing but just enough."

Eleanor looked slightly concerned, "Don't overdo it Gilbert. It could all blow up in your face."

He calmed her, "We have to start somewhere. I want people to be intrigued enough to go out and buy the book. I'm not suggesting for one moment that I admit to being a lunatic."

She relaxed a bit, "Of course not. My advice is to let the story seep out in to people's consciousness. Let them come to the conclusions that you want to. Rather than state the facts, give them clues."

Gilbert nodded, "Don't worry. That is exactly what I intend to do."

They walked across the courtyard and entered the Royal Academy. Gilbert imagined that he was Turner or Constable, coming to see one of their own paintings hanging at an exhibition.

"I am very proud of you, Monsieur," said a very small voice at his side. He smiled and gave her the thumbs up.

The painting had been hung in the gallery normally reserved for the summer exhibition and it had been given pride of place. Gilbert was delighted. It looked good.

When the reporter from the BBC arrived, she was effusive in her compliments.

"I think this is a great scene. It is the type of print that I like to hang in my living room."

Gilbert was grateful, "Thank you, Laura. I'll make sure that you get a print. I'll even sign it for you."

Laura laughed, "Another offer, I can't refuse."

The BBC set up their camera and it wasn't long before he was being interviewed for BBC News.

"First of all, congratulations on your win in the Trinity Prize. On the night, you told me that the painting was the story of a broken heart. Can you give us a few more details?"

Gilbert smiled. He felt comfortable in front of the camera, "Thirty-five years ago, this June, I visited Châtelaillon-Plage, whilst on holiday in Charente-Maritime.

When I was there, I spent the day with a girl who introduced herself as Margaux. Before I left, she handed me a note with her address. I wrote to her but unfortunately, she never replied. I have wondered ever since what happened to her."

"She must have had quite an impact on you?"

Gilbert raised his eyebrows, "That is an understatement. I have dreamt about her almost every night since I returned and there are a few reasons for that. In hindsight, when I look back at the events of that day, it felt like Margaux had been waiting for me. Not only that, I had the funniest feeling that I had met her before. I can't put my finger on it, but it felt like something mysterious had happened and I have always been greatly intrigued by it."

Laura shivered, "You have a habit of giving your readers

goose-bumps. Can we expect the novel to be a scary story?"

Gilbert laughed, "It isn't a ghost story or a horror. It is an attempt to find out who Margaux really is. Why was she waiting for me on the beach that day? Why didn't she write back?"

Laura stepped up to the painting, "I see you've painted the children sharing an ice-cream. Did you consciously make it ambiguous?"

Gilbert looked perplexed, "What do you mean, ambiguous?"

Laura faltered slightly, and she looked at him with a frown, "It is not clear which child is which. Who is Margaux?"

Gilbert felt himself go white in the face. He walked up to the canvas, "Margaux is the one facing the camera, as it were. She is handing me the ice cream. I have my back turned."

Laura chuckled, "It wasn't clear. You are both wearing the same tee shirt and shorts."

Gilbert's stomach did a somersault. He looked again, "Well, I'll be damned."

Laura looked concerned, "Are you alright, Mr Martin?"

Gilbert looked in to space, "Sweet Jesus Christ."

Laura pulled herself together, "Mr Martin. I can't wait to read your book." She turned to the camera, "Châtelaillon-Plage is out in bookshops this Friday priced at £14.99. You better make sure you are in the queue as I can see this selling out very quickly. This was Laura Kuenssberg, for BBC news at the Royal Academy."

The camera stopped rolling. Laura turned to him, "That was absolutely superb, Mr Martin. You even managed to scare the devil out of me."

Gilbert was still in a daze. He looked again at the painting. How could something so obvious, that had taken him seven months to paint, pass him by so completely.

Eleanor came over to thank the BBC reporter, "Sorry, Laura, I think he's having one of his moments. He quite often does things without realising he's done them. I don't think he noticed that he'd painted the children wearing the same thing."

Laura looked intrigued, "Yes. I certainly got that impression. He seems a bit shocked."

Gilbert was shocked. In fact, he was frightened. The realisation that he and Margaux had been wearing the same thing on the beach had given him quite a turn. The conversation they had shared that day came back to him.

"My name is Margaux Martin. What's yours?"

"My name is Gilbert Martin. We are both the same."

She had smiled and looked pleased, "Obviously. I think we are married. Do you want to kiss the bride?"

He felt a little hand clasp his own, "Please don't be afraid. There is nothing to worry about. I always knew that we were the same. I waited for you a long time and now, I will never let you go."

He squeezed her hand in response, "I am very glad to hear it, Madam."

V

Châtelaillon-Plage

Friday morning arrived with the omen of uncommonly good weather. It was the sun that had awoken him. His bed was situated opposite the window and it was the heat that he had noticed first.

"Wake up, Monsieur. Today is the big day."

He climbed out of bed and walked in to the shower. When he was done, she was waiting with a towel, "I have laid out your good suit and I have polished your black shoes. Hurry, the taxi will be here in twenty minutes."

He had taken the liberty of booking the cab the night before. He wanted to be at the hotel in plenty of time.

When he was ready to leave, she was waiting at the door, "Good luck, Monsieur. Don't let me down."

He knelt down and kissed her on the cheek, "Letting you down is the last thing I will ever do. I have prepared for this day for a long time. Don't worry. I am ready".

He opened the door and jumped in to the waiting taxi.

The room was packed. Gilbert's performance on television had ensured there were no empty seats for the launch of his new book "Châtelaillon-Plage". It was the same room in the Dorchester Hotel where he had received his prize for the painting. This had been Eleanor's idea, "They will make a connection between the painting and the book, trust me, it will be worth the extra expense."

Gilbert smiled. It was curious how often she turned out to be right.

The room quietened, and Gilbert could see that the reporter from the BBC, Laura, was already standing.

"Mr Martin, thank you for letting me have the first question. Can you tell us what the book is really about? You have given us some great clues, but I'd be grateful for a little more detail as to what the driving force behind it is and where it is going to take us?"

Gilbert laughed and nodded, "You ask questions that go on for miles. I'll try to answer as best I can.

The driving force behind the book is the question of my mental health. Thirty-five years ago, I met a girl on a beach in France who made a lasting impression on me. We clicked, but it was more than that. I felt that I'd been waiting to meet her, just as she had been waiting to meet me.

When I left the beach that day, I came away with more than her address. Of course, I wrote to her on several occasions but she, for some unknown reason, did not write back.

I was not completely unsurprised by this on account of the fact that Margaux has been with me ever since. I have not only felt her presence, over the years, I have fallen in to the mental health trap of talking to her. She is, to all intents and purposes, with me every day.

I know a lot of you will find this hard to believe but she is as real to me as a member of my own family. I chat to her and she answers back.

Obviously, I have raised the issue with my GP and have been referred to a psychiatrist, but no medication seems to resolve the issue. The book is my way of dealing with the problem once and for all.

Did something mysterious happen on that beach and if it did can I use the book to find out? Or, am I simply mentally ill and need to resolve the issue by other means?

In the book, I have explored the possibility of one conclusion, but this is a fiction. I am merely using that as a means to an end. I am asking my readers to help me find out what happened to Margaux Martin and what happened to me."

There was complete and utter silence in the room.

The BBC reporter hesitated before she plunged ahead, "Are you saying that you have been in the company of... er... a ghost, for thirty-five years."

There was absolutely no tittering or exchanged glances.

Gilbert chuckled, "I know this is difficult, but the experience is very real. I don't know if Margaux is a ghost. My worst fear is that something bad happened to her that day and she decided to come home with me. If that is the case, then, with your help, I can find out in France."

Laura looked at him quizzically, "But you're not ruling it out?"

Gilbert folded his hands in front of him, "No. I'm ruling nothing out. I have lived with Margaux for such a long time now that I keep an open mind as to every possibility. I think there are several possible explanations.

One. I have a mental health problem which needs to be resolved.

Two. Margaux died that day and somehow her spirit followed me home to Scotland.

Three. There is an unexplained connection between me and Margaux that transcends our normal human capabilities and needs to be explored.

Four. Margaux is not human.

Five. There is an explanation that I've not considered because it is so far out there, it has not even occurred to me."

Laura hesitated again. She looked at him apologetically, "I'm sorry if this offends but I'm afraid I've got to ask the question. Do you think that you are mentally ill?"

Gilbert smiled at her, "Thank you for being kind. I do not believe that I am mentally ill. I know I'm different, but you would know that if you had read any of my books. I think that I am as sound as a pound."

Every single person in the room was rapt. A middle-aged man in a scruffy suit stood up, "Mr Martin, I'm from The Guardian. Can you tell me what you know about Margaux so that I can help you? I will put all the details you know in an article for the paper and will happily publish."

There were lots of nods around the room.

Gilbert looked at them all gratefully, "Thank you, Sir. This is what I know for certain.

In 1983, Margaux was thirteen and thinks she was born in 1970.

She says she comes from the town of Margaux in Haut-Medoc, where the famous wine is made.

She lived in a one storey cottage on the Rue Jeanne D'Arc.

Her father owned a Citroen DS.

When I saw her on Châtelaillon-Plage, she was with someone she called "Maman".

That is all I know but I think it is a good start."

A young woman of about twenty-five stood up, "Can you see her? Is she now forty-eight years old? Is she with you now?"

Gilbert laughed. The question had caused a bit of tension and he felt the need to lighten the mood, "I can see her as clear as day. She appears as she did in 1983 and she usually stays at home. If she pays me a visit, I normally see a flash of white light and she is there at my side."

The woman wasn't finished, "Why don't you just ask her what happened?"

There were a few tuts in the crowd.

Gilbert raised his eyebrows, "She can't remember very much. She says that most things are a blank. She remembers being on the beach with me and the next thing she remembers is being in my hotel room in La Rochelle. I've told you all I know."

Laura stood up again, "You say that one of the possibilities you have considered is that Margaux may not be human. Can you expand on that? What are your thoughts?"

Gilbert shrugged, "It has crossed my mind that she may be an awareness who wants to find out more about humankind. I can't rule out the possibility because the experience has been so strange. She has always told me that we are the same and that she had been waiting for me.

Over the years, I have tried to understand what she means by "we are the same". I have concluded that there is one thing that we both have in common. We are both very loving.

Is that the answer? Was she waiting for somebody who was very loving because she knew that she would be able to talk to them? Perhaps she tried with some others and they didn't match her requirements and then I came along, and she thought, now this is an idiot I can work with."

There was a huge outburst of laughter. The conversation had been getting tense and with that one statement, Gilbert had brought the room back to his side.

Laura finished chortling, "Okay, what are the next steps?"

Gilbert rubbed his hands, "I need you to publish kind articles on my behalf and then I go off to France and do the same thing there. I have an interview lined up, next Wednesday, on French television.

I'm hoping that social media will pick up on it and that I'll get a bit of traction. Once that happens then I can go down to Bordeaux and do a bit of digging. Who knows? In a week or two weeks, I might have the answers I've been looking for all my adult life."

Laura nodded and smiled, "Good luck, Mr Martin. I hope you aren't just mad because, if that is the case, then I'm going to be one very disappointed reporter."

They all laughed again but stood up and gave him a standing ovation.

When the noise died down, he turned to Eleanor, "That wasn't so bad, was it?"

She was smiling from ear to ear, "Gilbert, my darling, that was sheer bloody dynamite."

When the crowd had drifted off, Gilbert asked Eleanor if she would like a glass of wine.

She made a face, "It's a bit early for me."

He winked, "Trust me. It is never too early for this."

He went in to his bag and pulled out a bottle of the 1983 Chateau Margaux, "I'm serving this on Saturday for dinner. My birthday, however, was yesterday and I still haven't had the opportunity to have a drink with anyone."

She put on her glasses, "Well, I never. The 1983 Margaux. You are so incredibly thoughtful."

Gilbert uncorked the bottle with his Swiss Army knife, "The wonderful co-incidence is that Chateau Margaux just happens to be one of the five Bordeaux wines which were granted premier cru status by the 1855 classification system. It is la crème de la crème."

He picked up two wine glasses from a nearby table and poured out generous helpings. She sipped the wine, "Oh my God. That is sublime. It is, without doubt, the best wine I have ever tasted."

Gilbert smirked, "By a further lucky co-incidence, 1983 was a vintage year. It is la crème de la crème de la crème".

She looked at him curiously, "Sometimes this whole thing gives me a supernatural thrill. I'm just not surprised that Margaux is a premier cru. I'm not surprised that 1983 is a vintage year. Do you ever feel like the fates are following you?"

He laughed, "All the time. There is nothing about this business that surprises me anymore. I wouldn't be surprised if I got to France and found Margaux's father, found that he still drove the Citroen and that he'd called it Gilbert since the day he had bought it."

Eleanor coughed and looked at him with a frightened expression, "You don't think he did, do you?"

He stared at her with a twilight zone expression, "Who can say? Who can say? Ha, ha. Ha. Ha. Ha."

She laughed, "You are incorrigible. What do you think you are going to find there?"

He thought for a moment, "I think I am going to find a resolution. One way or another, I will resolve my issues."

She raised her glass, "I'll drink to that. To a resolution."

He followed suit, "To a resolution."

VI

Bon Anniversaire

"When are they due to arrive?"

Gilbert stirred the pot of home-made French onion soup, "They are due to arrive at 7.00 for drinks and then we'll sit round for dinner at 7.30."

She sat at the breakfast bar looking nervous, "I'm worried, Monsieur. What if they make fun of us?"

Gilbert smiled to calm her, "Eleanor and Savannah will not make fun of us. I haven't met their husbands but if they are a problem then I give you full authority to deal with them. You may give them what for."

The nervous look became a wicked smile, "Are you sure, Monsieur?"

He nodded, "Listen, Margaux, I'm as tired of all this as you are. I just want a happy life and I can't have that if you are a secret, hidden away all the time. It's time we asserted ourselves."

She sniffed the air, "It smells very good."

He laughed, "I'm not surprised. It's your recipe."

He stirred the pot once again and when he turned back there was a gift-wrapped parcel on the breakfast bar, "What's this?"

She smiled enigmatically, "Bon Anniversaire, ma Chérie."

He kissed her cheek, "Merci, Madame." He peeled back the wrapping paper and found a black velvet necklace box. He opened it. Inside was a silver chain with little silver letters dangling from it. It read "TROUVE-MOI".

He was speechless, "How did you manage this?"

She shrugged, "I ordered it on the internet, using your credit card."

He chuckled, "I love it. Help me put it on."

She stood on a stool and fastened the necklace at the back of his neck. He could clearly see the lettering through his open necked shirt.

"C'est parfait, Monsieur."

There was a knock on the door. Gilbert put his hand on her cheek, "Now be calm. It is all going to be okay."

He went to the door. They had all arrived together and they had all been drinking. Gilbert suspected that Eleanor was behind this. It would give her a chance to brief everybody before they came to the house. She introduced her partner, "This is Dennis".

Dennis was a big man with a beard and a kind face, "How do you do, Gilbert?"

He smiled. Dennis wouldn't be a problem, "I'm very well, thank you."

Dr Wilde introduced her husband, the attorney, "This is Peter."

Gilbert looked the man up and down. He was tall, trim, and clean shaven. Gilbert felt like he was a man who tolerated no nonsense. His expression was cynical. Better try to keep him on side.

"Nice to meet you, Peter."

"And you, Gilbert." He held out his hand and Gilbert performed the firm hand shake.

Dr Wilde kissed him on the cheek and handed over a small gift, "Happy birthday, Gilbert."

He looked at the parcel curiously, "Thank you. Do I open it now?"

She laughed, "Yes please."

He ripped open the gift to find a small box. Inside was a compass.

"In case you get lost, you can always find your way home."

Gilbert was touched. It was a lovely gift, "Thank you, Savannah."

He took their coats and hanged them up in the hall cupboard, "We may as well go through to the dining room. The first course is more or less ready to serve."

They made their way through to the dining room and sat down at the table. There were six places.

Peter looked at the extra setting, "Are we expecting someone else?"

Gilbert smiled at him, "She's here already. I'll get the soup."

Gilbert went through to the kitchen and transferred the contents of the pot in to the soupier, "I don't like him," She said.

Gilbert winked at her, "He'll be fine. This is just a bit odd for him. I promise it will be ok."

He carried the soupier through to the dining room and laid it on the table, "Ladies and gentlemen. I give you French onion soup. Please help yourself."

His guests were obviously famished and attacked the soupier. Soon everyone had a full bowl.

Savannah took a spoonful, "This is delicious. Not everyone can make a bowl of genuine French onion soup."

Gilbert laughed, "It is Margaux's recipe".

Peter was looking at the empty place setting, "Is she here, now?"

Gilbert nodded, "Yes. She is here at the table."

Peter put his spoon down in the bowl. He looked directly at Gilbert, "I don't mind telling you that this is a bit odd. Savannah has asked me to be your attorney should you encounter any problems but trust me, it's a bit easier to perform that task if you are a believer. I'm not the believer type and this looks distinctly silly. From a position in court perspective, I think I would have trouble defending you."

Gilbert nodded. He wasn't surprised, "I understand your perspective. Give it a bit of time."

Peter was about to say something else when the spoon in the dish did a summersault of its own volition. Hot soup was sprayed over his face and shirt.

"Jesus Christ." He jumped back, away from the table.

Eleanor, Dennis, and Savannah started tittering.

Gilbert shrugged, "No, Peter, not Jesus Christ. Margaux Martin, at your service." He started to laugh.

Peter was looking less sure of himself. He pulled his chair back under the table and looked down at his bowl.

Gilbert leaned over, "This could get very much worse, very quickly, unless you start believing very soon."

Peter looked up "Is this your idea of a joke? How did you do that?"

Gilbert sat back in his seat and held his arms up in the air, "I'm not doing anything."

The bowl in front of Peter suddenly took a leap and landed in his lap, scalding his nether regions and thighs, "Jesus Fucking Christ."

Everybody started to laugh.

Peter stood up. He checked his table setting for strings or other hidden devices, "What is going on?"

Gilbert held his hand up to calm him, "Margaux does not like your attitude. I suggest you calm down and behave a little bit better."

Peter picked up the bowl and looked at it. He put it down on the table and sat back down on his chair. He looked around the room, "Okay. I agree to behave. Just don't cover me in any more soup."

He helped himself to another portion from the soupier. He was smiling.

Gilbert explained, "Margaux doesn't like any disparagement whatsoever. Trust me, she is very real, and I am definitely not mad."

Peter looked at him ruefully, "I accept that she is real, and you are not mad. Why can't we see her?"

Gilbert shook his head, "I genuinely don't know. On the day I met her she told me that we were both the same. I still don't really know what that means. She may have meant that we both have the same set of skills that mean we can speak to each other. I simply have no idea."

Peter nodded, "Okay, I'm in. I am officially intrigued by this case. Not just because I have been covered in French onion soup but because I can actually sense her presence. I can feel her in the room."

Gilbert was shocked, "Are you sure?"

Eleanor leaned forward, "So, can I."

Dennis and Savannah both nodded their heads, "I can feel her too," they said in unison.

Gilbert could have cried, "Well, I'll be damned."

Savannah finished her soup, "I think I could do with a glass of wine."

Gilbert jumped. He had forgotten the Chateau Margaux, "Of course. I think you'll like this one. I have managed to get several bottles of the Chateau Margaux 1983 in memory of the year we met."

He went to the dresser and picked up one of the opened bottles and poured them all a glass.

Peter took a sip, "It is exquisite. A real vintage wine."

Gilbert agreed, "Yes. I don't actually remember tasting a better one. I think it is officially my favourite."

"I think we are making progress, Monsieur," said Margaux.

There was utter silence in the room. Eleanor stopped with the glass midway to her mouth.

Dennis was looking round the room.

Peter turned to Gilbert, "I take it, we have just heard the voice of Margaux Martin?"

Gilbert couldn't believe it, "Yes, that was Margaux. She thinks we are making progress".

Peter nodded, "Yes. We heard." He looked at the empty seat, "Thank you for inviting us to your birthday party."

"You are welcome, Monsieur. Sorry for covering you in soup."

Everyone laughed, "Don't worry. I'm just glad that we are able to talk to you at last."

There was silence, "I think you have always been able to talk to me. I think you have to make a choice. I think that's how our brains work. If you don't make the choice, then you can't perform the task."

Peter pursed his lips, "That is interesting. I would like to ask you a few questions, but I am fearful of offending you."

"You may ask. I will not be offended."

"Do you know who you are?"

They could all feel a sense of amusement in the room, "Yes. I know who I am, but you have to do what is on Gilbert's necklace. When you do that, all will become clear."

They all looked at Gilbert who was in a state of shock, "What is on your necklace?" asked Peter.

Gilbert opened his shirt so that they could see, "It was a birthday present from Margaux."

They looked at the tiny lettering, "TROUVE-MOI."

"What does it mean?" asked Dennis.

Gilbert looked at him, "It means "FIND ME"."

Peter looked over at the empty seat, "What do you mean by that?"

There was no answer. Gilbert looked at Peter, "She has left the room, but she is happy."

Peter nodded, "At least we can rule out the madness theory. You are definitely not mad."

Gilbert smiled, "Thanks. But I knew that already."

Eleanor took a sip of her wine, "She's not a ghost. She is not dead, and she is asking you to find her. I think we can rule out the ghost theory."

Gilbert frowned, "I think I agree with you. I'm not ruling it out completely, but my instincts tell me that you are correct. She is not a ghost."

Savannah clasped her hands, "What does that leave?"

Gilbert shifted in his seat, "Margaux is not human or there is an unexplained connection between the two of us."

Peter looked up, "Or there is something that you have not considered yet."

Gilbert nodded, "I agree. There could be something that I haven't thought of."

Dennis, who had been very quiet, joined in the conversation, "If I was alien and wanted to find out more about the human race, I think I might use the innocence of a child to find out what I wanted."

The rest of the group nodded but Gilbert intervened, "I can't rule that out, but it feels wrong. When I was on the beach, somebody called out to her and she said it was Maman. I don't think she is alien. There is something that I'm missing. Something that I've always missed."

They continued their conversation through the main course of Parmentier de Veaux. A veal stew with mashed potatoes and a mustard gelatine. When it came to dessert, Gilbert went off to find Margaux. She was in the bedroom.

"You are going to miss out on your Rum Baba with Sauce Malaga."

She giggled, "You save me one. My work for today is done. I have given you all the clues that I can and if I come through, they will just ask me more questions. You know what to do now and things have been set up nicely to help you do the thing that you must do before it is too late."

He looked worried, "What's that, my love?"

"Find me."

VII

The Twitterati

The large suitcase was almost full.
"Do you want to take your walking shoes?"
Gilbert thought about it for a moment, "Yes, I think so. Let's put them in the little bags that came with the brogues."
Margaux put the shoes in to little cotton drawstring bags that had been provided with a pair of brogues they had bought on the internet.
"I think that's you nearly packed. What time is your taxi?"
Gilbert smiled, "It is not until 11.30 in the morning. We have time for a few glasses of wine. We still haven't opened the 1970."
She sighed, "Don't get too drunk. We'll have the one bottle and then straight to bed. I don't want you missing your flight."
He lifted her up in to his arms, "I won't miss my flight and I won't get drunk. This is too important to make any mistakes."
She kissed him, "I'm glad you are taking it seriously."
They zipped up the suitcase and placed it at the front door with his hand luggage.
Gilbert opened the 1970 and poured out two glasses, "Pour vous, Madame."
She took the proffered glass and sat down on the sofa, "Merci à vous, Monsieur."
Gilbert sipped his wine. It wasn't as good as the '83 but it

wasn't bad either. Silky and sweet, "This is a pleasant surprise. I hadn't expected it to be as good."

Margaux sniffed and nodded, "It is the time that has made it. We are probably drinking it at exactly the right moment. For me, it is perfect."

They sat quietly for a few minutes before Gilbert plucked up the courage to ask the question which had been nagging at him, "What did you mean, the other night, when you said I had to find you before it was too late?"

She screwed her face up, "I didn't mean to worry you. That was not my intention. I am here and I am not here. I find it difficult to explain. All I know is that you must find me soon, otherwise I will have run out of time."

He frowned, "You are scaring me."

She nodded, "I know, but you need to use your fear as an incentive. You have been asleep for far too long and now I have woken you up. I wouldn't have bothered if it had not been urgent but I had no choice. They are calling me and if my time runs out then I will have to go."

He took another sip of his wine, "Who is calling you?"

She looked sad, "There are those who will not see me stranded. They will not see anybody stranded here. I cannot tell you who they are because I don't know. I can hear their voices and they are getting louder."

Gilbert put down his glass and lifted up his i Pad, "Eleanor has been trying to get a hashtag trending on twitter. It is called #findme. She has told our story using the book launch as a cover. She promised that she would vet all the replies and then send me e-mails if there are any clues worth following up."

Margaux sat up in her seat, "Are there any?"

Gilbert smiled, "We already have eight e-mails."

Gilbert looked at the first one. It was from a woman from Cantanac called Elise Simon, "This woman remembers a

Margaux that she went to school with. She doesn't give any dates though nor does she give an address."

Margaux laughed, "I think you are going to get a lot of that. Margaux is not a totally uncommon name."

Gilbert went through the e-mails, "There's nothing here that I would actually call a lead. It's just a load of people who knew a Margaux when they were teenagers."

She jumped off her seat, "When you get to France, you can use your television interview to get people to give you more details. Contact information etcetera. Don't get disheartened on me."

He lifted her up in to a cuddle, "I won't get disheartened. I'm not coming home until I've found you."

She kissed him, "Make sure you don't."

The following morning, they both got up early and had a long hearty breakfast. There were lots of tears and warnings to be careful. When it was time to leave, Gilbert stood at the door and did a last check.

"Euros, check, bank cards, check, airline ticket, check. Is there anything I've forgotten?"

She shook her head, "Passport?"

He put his hand to his mouth, "Oh my God. It was in the package Mum sent down from Scotland."

Margaux sighed, "It is in the dresser drawer."

He went through to the dining room and pulled the package from the dresser drawer. He retrieved his passport and put it in his jacket pocket, "Right. I'm ready to go. Wish me luck, Madame."

"Bonne chance, ma Chérie. Bonne chance."

He kissed her goodbye. Picked up his bags and went out to the taxi. He jumped in the cab and asked the driver to take him to Gatwick.

He settled back in his seat and picked up his iPad. He started looking at the e-mails Eleanor had sent through.

There was an update on the one from Elise Simon.

Gilbert, I contacted Elise Simon and asked her to give more detail. I think you will be interested in the response.

Gilbert opened the attachment and read the e-mail which had been sent by Elise under the subject #findme.

Dear Eleanor

My name is Elise Simon. In 1983, I lived in the village of Cantanac in Gironde.

I knew a Margaux Martin from our days at Ecole de Margaux. We had our enseignement primaire at this school.

We were supposed to go to the Lycée together but she and her family disappeared during the summer. I did not hear from her after that and there was no news.

I am sorry to say that I did not travel from my village to find out what happened to her and this is all I know. I started my enseignement secondaire in 1983.

Elise Simon

Gilbert whistled. He had to admit that there were definite possibilities. He didn't want to get too excited. Margaux was not an unpopular name and Martin was the most popular surname in France. He decided to ask Eleanor to write to Elise again and ask for a photograph. That would remove any doubt. He wrote the e-mail.

By the time he had sent it, they were on the M25, just south of Windsor. The taxi driver looked in his rear-view mirror and asked the question he had been working himself up to ask for about 15 minutes, "Any luck yet, mate?"

Gilbert smiled, "I've had some positive responses and one good lead. I'm on my way to France now to follow up on it."

The taxi driver looked somewhat relieved, "Well I hope you find her soon. My wife is going daft over the whole thing. She's been mooning about the house checking her iPhone every ten minutes to see if there are any updates."

Gilbert was delighted and surprised, "I'm afraid I don't do twitter very much. Are you getting the sense that people are engaging in the campaign?"

The driver laughed, "Engaging. The whole country is completely intrigued by it. I'm intrigued by it and I don't believe in any nonsense. I think you've managed to get everybody thinking. You've portrayed it as a mystery rather than a ghost story and I think that's been the winning strategy."

Gilbert sat back in his seat, "It is a bloody mystery. I just wish I could solve it. Do you have a theory, yourself?"

The man frowned, "I like the idea of a non-corporeal entity. Who is to say that every sentience in the universe has to have a body like ours?

I wouldn't really have given it much thought had it not been for the cloud. I store all my music albums in the apple iCloud. Twenty-five years ago, they were all records on my shelf.

What if the universe has a thing similar to the cloud where sentient beings essentially live? Their awarenesses can travel but they ultimately have a home, not in cyberspace but in actual space?"

Gilbert's face went white, "Gosh, I never thought about it like that but you're right, why can't the universe have that capability? Take it one step further. What if we all end up in the cloud?"

The driver nodded, "It's funny you should say that because that is exactly what I thought. It is the next natural step."

Gilbert leaned back and closed his eyes. He could see exactly where the driver was coming from and it made complete sense to him when he thought about the behaviour of Margaux. She could appear out of nowhere at the drop of a hat. She came when he called.

"What are you thinking?" asked the driver.

Gilbert smiled, "I think I've just gone to the next step. What if there are human beings who have the capability, without realising it, to summon these entities from the cloud?"

The driver's eyebrows shot up, "That would explain those that have genuine capabilities as mediums. Is that what you think you are doing?"

Gilbert shrugged, "I've no idea but I wouldn't rule it out. It really makes quite a lot of sense when I think about it."

The driver chuckled, "I could talk to you all day about this but I'm afraid we're coming up to the airport. I think you've got your work cut out but I wish you the very best of luck in your search."

Gilbert was grateful, "Thank you."

When they reached the terminal, Gilbert said goodbye and gave the driver a generous tip.

"Good luck, again." He drove off and Gilbert lifted his bags and walked in to the terminal.

He found the queue for Charles de Gaulle and checked in. He was flying to Paris and then taking the train to La Rochelle. When he got to la Rochelle he would hire a car and just see where his investigations took him.

He checked in his suitcase and headed for the departure lounge for a sandwich. When he was seated with a cheese and ham baguette and a cup of coffee, he opened his iPad. There was a response from Eleanor.

Hi Gilbert
Elise Simon has been in touch to say she had a photograph of the Margaux she knew. It's a digital photograph of the original image and is attached to this e mail. Just click on the icon.

Gilbert clicked on the icon and let the image load up on the screen.

It was a little bit grainy but depicted two girls of about thirteen with their arms about each other. They appeared to be in the car park at a swimming pool. They were both smiling.

Gilbert looked at the girl on the left and felt the hairs at the back of his neck stand on end. She was wearing a black denim jacket and black jeans. His heart did a summersault. He had owned exactly the same jacket and jeans at that age. Exactly the same.

When he looked at the face, there was no doubt about it. Staring back at him was his Margaux Martin. She was a bit younger but it was definitely her.

The picture was making his skin come out in goose bumps. He knew it was there, in front of him but he couldn't see it. What was he missing? There was something about this image that was so profound that he ought to be able to click his fingers and draw a conclusion.

He wrote back to Eleanor.

Eleanor

It's her. No doubt about it. Can you arrange a meeting with Elise?

Gilbert took a sip of his coffee and heard that voice once more, "We are the same, Monsieur."

VIII

Paris

When Gilbert Martin put his foot on the tarmac at Charles de Gaulle airport, he felt that familiar thrill he always felt when he arrived in France. One word jumped in to his mind. Home.

He walked across the tarmac to the waiting shuttle and stepped on to the bus. Within 25 minutes, he was at the front of the taxi rank loading the back seat of his cab with his luggage.

"Rue de Courcelles, s'il vous plait, Monsieur."

The taxi driver looked at him, "L'hotel Collectionneur?"

He nodded, "Oui, s'il vous plâit."

He sat back in his seat and closed his eyes. He loved this part of the journey. He liked to savour the smell of France. The light, he had noticed years ago, was different. He allowed the vermillion glow to permeate his eyelids. It gave him a sense of deep emotional happiness. He fell asleep.

When he awoke, he was outside the hotel. He paid the taxi driver and allowed the concierge to help him with his luggage.

L'hotel Collectionneur was a tribute to the art déco style. The reception reminded him of the 1930's. He had chosen the hotel quite deliberately as the bedrooms were vast and the bathrooms luxurious. Who didn't want to get ready for dinner in a marble encased shrine to a decadent world that had long gone?

He stepped up to reception and checked in, "Welcome to the Collectionneur, Mr Martin, it is nice to see you again."

Gilbert nodded. He enjoyed the fact that the hotel system recorded his previous stays, "Thank you. It is good to be back."

He was given the electronic key card to room 83. He smiled. The year he met Margaux. Eleanor had asked him if he felt the fates were following him. They clearly were.

The rooms were just as he remembered them. Vast, sumptuous, and stylish. He hung up a few suits and repaired to the bathroom for a wash and brush up. He opened his toilet bag and pulled out the after-shave Margaux had packed for him. It was Boucheron. As far as he was concerned, the best Paris had to offer. He used it lavishly.

As he walked back in to the bedroom, his phone rang. He picked up the device and swiped to accept the call, "Hello. Gilbert Martin speaking."

"Hi Gilbert, it's Eleanor. How was your flight?"

He sat on the bed, "Very comfortable as usual. I enjoy the Air France sandwiches. You never quite know what you're going to get."

She chuckled, "You and your stomach. I have some news for you. Elise Simon has agreed to meet you and the good thing is, she lives in Paris now. Do you know the Avenue Hoche?"

Gilbert nearly fell off the bed, "Yes. I know it well. It's just around the corner."

Eleanor was silent for a moment, "Quelle surprise. I don't mind telling you, Gilbert. The more I get in to this, the scarier it gets. There are so many co-incidences, it's frightening."

Gilbert chuckled, "Tell me about it. I've been thinking about it a lot and I'm pretty sure it's Margaux. I think she is perfectly capable of arranging these little incidents. She can pretty much go where she pleases when she puts her mind to it."

Eleanor snorted, "She couldn't have arranged for Elise Simon to live on the Avenue Hoche."

Gilbert laughed, "No, but she could arrange for me to stay in a hotel around the corner in room 83, which, if you will recall, was the year we met."

Eleanor sighed, "Good point. She could have arranged that. What do you want me to say to Elise Simon?"

Gilbert thought about it for a moment, "Tell her to meet me in the hotel reception at 1.00 tomorrow for lunch and ask her to bring the photograph and anything else that is relevant."

"Right, will do. What are you doing now? Are you going out for dinner?"

He made a "doh" sound, "Of course, I'm going out for dinner. I'm in Paris. I think I might head on over to Pierre Gagnaire. It is expensive but I can afford it after all."

She sounded jealous, "You lucky thing. Enjoy yourself. In the meantime, I'll get in touch with Elise."

Gilbert said goodbye, put the phone on the inside pocket of his jacket and headed for the elevator.

As he got to the end of the corridor, the lift juddered to a halt and he stepped inside. He pressed the button for the ground floor. Almost immediately, there was a familiar flash of bright white light and she was standing beside him. She put her hand in his.

"What brings you to Paris, Madame?"

She smiled up at him, "Time is running out, ma Chérie. If you are going to a three-star Michelin restaurant, I thought it would be a good idea to come with you so that I can at least experience the pleasure once in my life".

Gilbert felt himself go cold all over, "What do you mean, time is running out?"

She looked at him sadly, "They keep calling me now. I am finding it harder to resist. It is my belief that you must be successful or I won't be able to hold them off."

He knelt down and looked in to her eyes, "Who is calling you, Margaux?"

She did not look afraid, "There is nothing to be afraid of. The ones calling me love us very much. I think they are making a contingency should you be unable to find me. They know you just as much as they know me. Remember, we are the same, Monsieur. We always have been."

An image jumped in to his mind. Two girls standing in a swimming pool car park. One girl, he didn't know but the other was wearing his jacket and jeans. We are both the same. What was he missing?

He looked at Margaux again, "Do you remember Elise Simon?"

She smiled, "Yes. We were good friends. I remember her very well."

Gilbert put his hands on her shoulders, "She sent me a photograph of the two of you visiting a swimming pool when you were young. I've seen the image but there is something that I'm missing. I can't quite put my finger on it."

The look Margaux gave him could only be translated as one of triumph, "You are getting there, Monsieur. Let me give you a clue. The question you must ask Elise is this. How did you get to the swimming pool and how did you get home? The answer is there in front of you."

Gilbert started to feel a bit better, "I think you know more than you are letting on?"

She laughed, "I love you. Life with you is perfect. If a girl wants to play hide and seek then you always indulge."

He sighed, "Are you really in trouble?"

She winked at him, "Not when I have someone as clever as you. I think you will work it out and we will be fine."

The lift door opened and they walked out, hand in hand, in to reception. When they got outside, Gilbert called a cab.

They jumped in.

"Pierre Gagnaire, s'il vous plait. Rue de Balzac."

The taxi driver looked at him like he was an idiot, "Je sais où est Pierre Gagnaire. Je viens de Paris."

Gilbert tittered and offered his apologies. They headed down the Rue de Courcelles in the late afternoon sunshine. Gilbert loved this time of day in Paris. The light shone brightly on the stone and brought out the subtle colours of Paris. Muted peach, shades of pastel green and shimmering vermillion.

They turned right on to the Rue de Monceau. Gilbert remembered that this street was once called the Rue Cisalpine. He wondered if it had been named after the Napoleonic client kingdom of the southern Alps. He guessed that it probably was. It was not long before they arrived at their destination.

The restaurant Pierre Gagnaire was housed in one of those magnificent streets built from white Lutetian Limestone that you find so often in Paris. Gilbert referred to this architecture as the embarrassment of riches. The sun imbued the stone with a pale-yellow colour that reminded him of gold sovereigns. They entered and waited for the Maître.

"Do you have a reservation, Monsieur?"

A small voice piped up, "Oui, au nom de Martin."

The waiter smiled, "Madame, Monsieur, suivez-moi."

They were led to a circular table in the corner of the restaurant. Gilbert pulled back the chair and let Margaux sit down, "Merci, Monsieur."

Gilbert moved round to his own place and sat down, being careful not to disturb the white table cloth, "What are you doing?" he whispered.

Margaux smiled with smug satisfaction, "I told you, Monsieur. I want to experience a three-star Michelin restaurant at least once in my life."

Gilbert raised an eyebrow, "I think I know you better than that. You are up to something. I can tell."

She laughed, "Well, of course, I am up to something. You have a date this evening and I wanted to make sure that you were here and prepared. This is extremely important. The person you are meeting has some information that you need. The more you impress her, the more talkative she will be. It will not be a bad idea to buy a really good bottle of wine from the menu and ply her with a few glasses. It will help loosen the tongue."

Gilbert was intrigued, "Who am I meeting?"

She smiled enigmatically, "You'll see."

It was dawning on him that Margaux was enjoying playing a game. He was not annoyed by this realisation, he was relieved. It meant that things were, perhaps, not as urgent as she had made out. If she wanted to be mysterious then he would indulge her. It would be worth it, as long as she was happy.

He picked up the menu, "Do you think we should order now or should we wait until she arrives?"

Margaux crossed her eyes, "She'll hardly thank you for being presumptuous enough to order on her behalf. Wait until she gets here."

Gilbert was curious, "How did you arrange this?"

Margaux laughed again. It was that silvery little melody that Gilbert loved so much, "I wondered when you would ask that question. I booked the restaurant weeks ago and I intercepted the e mail sent by Eleanor. I changed the time and date. Elise Simon is on her way here at this very moment. She is dying to meet you. Luckily, she has read your other books and will probably want your signature."

Gilbert nodded, "That won't be a problem. What are you going to do?"

Margaux made a face, "As much as I would like to stay

and meet an old friend, I think I will leave. It would be far too much for her."

He leaned back in his chair, "Okay, I understand. Is there anything that you particularly want me to ask her?"

She nodded in exasperation, "Just the obvious one we have already discussed. How did we get to the swimming pool and how did we get home?" Margaux stopped and looked nervously towards the door, "I'm going to have to leave you here. That is Elise just getting out of her taxi now. Good luck, Monsieur and don't forget to ask the right questions." With a flash of brilliant white light, she was gone.

The door to the restaurant opened and a slim woman aged about forty-eight walked in to the restaurant. She looked around and noticed Gilbert almost immediately. She smiled and headed straight for him.

"Bonjour, Monsieur. Je m'appelle Elise Simon."

Gilbert stood up and held out his hand, "Gilbert Martin. Thank you for coming Elise. Please take a seat."

She smiled her thanks and sat down opposite him, "You are very like my old friend Margaux, Monsieur."

IX

Elise Simon

Gilbert was a little bit disconcerted, "She is always telling me that we are the same. I don't know what she means by that but I never thought we looked like each other."

Elise Simon laughed, "Not necessarily look like. It is just that you are very alike. She was a happy gentle soul. Generous in every way. I get the feeling from reading your books that you are the same."

Gilbert was genuinely touched, "Thank you, Elise. What books of mine have you read."

She pulled a volume from her bag, "I have read them all but this is my favourite." She handed over a copy of "The Raft of the Medusa".

He was curious, "Why is this your favourite?"

She shifted in her seat, "I like how the story culminates in a visit to the Musée de Louvre and how you explain the painting. I actually agree with your interpretation of it. I wonder if you would sign it for me?"

Gilbert went in to his pocket and pulled out his silver Cross fountain pen, "Of course," he wrote a nice little inscription on the front page and handed it back.

Elise put the book back in her bag and pulled out a small folio which she placed at her side. She picked up the menu and started looking through the dishes, "I have eaten here once before and I heartily recommend the oysters to you."

Gilbert was deeply impressed, "Elise, your English is

magnificent. Where did you learn to speak so well?"

Elise Simon looked shocked, "From Margaux, of course. She was an excellent speaker. Her mother and her stepmother were both English, I think."

He suddenly had a very good feeling. He was speaking to someone who knew a lot more about Margaux's early life than he did. It was important that he asked as many questions as possible but not interrogate her so as to put her off.

He looked at her questioningly, "Her mother and stepmother?"

Elise nodded, "Yes. Margaux's real mother died when she was very young and her father re-married. In both cases, his wife was English. I always understood that her father was a bit of an anglophile. He loved the Rolling Stones and English punk music. He used to make us something called cottage pie. It was boeuf haché with mashed potatoes."

Gilbert smiled, "Yes. That is an all-time favourite. I wonder if that's what Margaux means when she says that we are both the same. I was brought up by my mother. My father died when I was two years old."

Elise shrugged, "It is possible. I know that she didn't get on with her stepmother. They were always fighting but she loved her father very much."

Gilbert picked up his menu, "Let's order. Pick a great wine and don't worry about the expense. This meal is on me."

Her face transformed, "If you say so, Monsieur. I have very expensive tastes."

Gilbert laughed, "So, have I."

They perused the menu and placed their orders when the waiter came over. Elise ordered for both of them.

"Nous voudrions grosse huître Tarbouriech, sirop de clémentine, pétales d'oignon doux; tout petit gigot d'agneau de Castille macéré dans un yaourt de brebis épicé. Le grand dessert. Pour vin, une bouteille de Chateau Haut-Brion 2012."

The waiter bowed, "Madame, Monsieur."

Gilbert looked at the folio Elise had laid on the table, "What have you brought with you?"

She picked up the folder and opened it, "I have brought some photographs with me. I don't have all that many. It is not like today when you can just snap someone with your phone. In those days, you had to go to a kodak shop and get your film developed".

She pulled out a small handful of photos, "This is the one I sent you." She handed over a large photograph of the her and Margaux taken in the swimming pool car park.

Gilbert trembled slightly as he held it in his hand, "Where was this taken, exactly?"

She thought about it for a moment, "That was taken in the summer of 1982, outside the piscine in Bordeaux. It was my twelfth birthday so it was July 21st."

Gilbert scrutinised the image, "How did you get to Bordeaux?"

Elise scratched her chin, "My father was away on business so my mother arranged a trip to Bordeaux with Margaux's father and stepmother. We went swimming and then shopping and after that we all went to a restaurant in Bordeaux called Le Chapon Fin. I think it is the oldest restaurant in the city."

Gilbert looked closely at the image. The girls were standing in front of a brown car. A Citroen DS. At last, the thing that had been escaping him heaved in to view. How had he missed it? "I take it that the car you are standing in front of is the car that belonged to Margaux's father"?

She looked at him strangely, "Yes. That is his car. How did you know that?"

He shrugged, "Margaux said that he had a Citroen DS and that everybody liked it."

She nodded in agreement, "Yes. Everybody loved that car. It is a classic."

Gilbert moved the photograph to the back of the pile and looked at the next one. It was a photograph of the girls and two adults at a restaurant table.

Elise leaned forward, "That is us at the restaurant later that day." She pointed her finger, "That is me, Margaux, my mother, and Margaux's father. Margaux's stepmother is taking the picture."

Gilbert looked at each person in turn. When he got to Margaux's father he felt his skin crawl and the hairs at the back of his neck stand on end. It couldn't be. It was impossible. He recognised the man in the photograph. His hair was bit longer but it was definitely him.

"Oh my God," said Gilbert.

"What is wrong?" enquired Elise. Her face was concerned.

Gilbert looked at her directly in the eye, "This man in the photograph. He is the spitting image of my dead father."

There was complete silence. She looked at him in complete shock. Eventually she murmured, "Are you sure?"

He nodded, "There is no doubt about it. It's him alright. My mother only had two photographs of him. One, on the day they were married and two, a photograph of him holding me as a baby. Although the photographs are older, there is no questioning the similarity. He is the exact same."

Elise thought about it for a moment, "Are you telling me that this man looks like your father or are you saying that he is your father."

Gilbert went white in the face, "Madame, there is no doubt. This man is my father. My mother told me that he was Scottish and died in an accident in the Royal Navy but here he is ten years after his death, living in the south of France."

Elise wouldn't let go, "What are you telling me, exactly, Monsieur?"

Gilbert shook his head, "I'm not sure. I think I'm telling

you that my mother has been lying to me all my life. What if they were married? What if my mother is Margaux's real mother who died? What if that's what Margaux meant all along when she said that we are the same. What if she meant that we were brother and sister?"

Suddenly, Elise Simon looked like a cat that had discovered a cream lake. She clicked her fingers in front of her face, "That's it. You are not brother and sister, Monsieur. You are twins."

Gilbert's stomach fell to the floor. Without knowing how she knew, he knew she was right. In fact, he had always known that this was the answer he had been waiting for all his adult life. The girl that he had shared his life with was the very same girl he had shared a womb with. There was no other explanation. They were too close to each other for there to be any other possibility. Margaux Martin was his twin. That was a fact.

Gilbert stared in to space, "Sweet Jesus. Sweet fucking Jesus."

Elise grabbed his hand across the table, "You know what this means, Monsieur. If you can find her father, then you can find out what happened to Margaux. In 1983, when she didn't appear at the Lycée, I have always regretted not trying to find out what happened to her. I made the assumption that she had simply moved away.

You can help me solve my conscience. I was lazy and too caught up in myself to worry about a friend. I would like to resolve that situation. If I can help you in any way, then I would like to."

Gilbert nodded, "Are you saying you want to come with me?"

She grinned, "That is exactly what I'm saying. I'm due leave from work. I can easily take two weeks off and take you down to Bordeaux. I know the area very well."

Gilbert put his hands on the table, "I think I would like that very much. Margaux has been telling me that there is a certain urgency about finding her. If we can find our father, then I agree with you. We can find her."

At that moment, the waiter appeared with two plates of oysters. He placed them down at their settings and opened the bottle of wine. He poured each of them a glass.

Elise Simon lifted her wine glass, "Here's to finding an old friend."

Gilbert clinked her glass and tasted the wine. It was outstanding, "I don't think I've ever tasted Haut-Brion."

Elise chuckled, "I'm letting you off lightly. Although this is expensive, a very good vintage would set you back about five thousand euros."

Gilbert started tucking in to his oysters, "What do you think we should do first? I have an interview tomorrow with French television and then I have a train booked to La Rochelle on Wednesday. I have a hotel there."

Elise thought about it for a moment, "I'll come with you on the train to La Rochelle. When we get there, we can decide a plan of action. It is only 2 hours to Margaux from there. We could easily hire a car."

Gilbert took a sip of his wine, "Fine. Let's do it that way. In the meantime, I will give my Mother a call to see what she has to say. You never know, she may have kept in touch with my father over the years. She might even know where he is."

Elise advised caution, "Be careful what you say. We have been sitting here making assumptions but we don't actually know the truth. You could go blundering in and ruin the whole thing. My advice is to simply state the facts and see what she says."

Gilbert thought that was good advice, "You are right of course. I have absolutely no idea if our assumptions are correct. Not only that, I have no idea why she might have left my father. I could be opening old wounds."

They finished their oysters and moved on to the lamb, Gilbert could easily see why this restaurant had three Michelin stars. The food was quite simply magnificent.

He looked across the table at his new friend, "Do you have room for grand dessert, whatever that is?"

She laughed, "I always have room for dessert. I don't think you will be disappointed."

Le Grand Dessert turned out to be separate tasting dishes of the most exquisite quality. When he was done, Gilbert felt like the fatted calf.

He sat back in his chair, "Wow. I think I've just eaten dinner of the year."

Elise opened her eyes wide, "Monsieur, I think you may have special powers. This has just been voted dinner of the year."

X

Interviews et enquêtes

As the taxi pulled up at the hotel, Gilbert agreed to meet Elise Simon in the hotel restaurant the following morning at 9.00. This would give her plenty of time to arrange time off work. He had an interview with French TV, in the morning and she also felt she could help with that.

In return, Gilbert agreed to arrange accommodation for her and buy train tickets. They would leave Gare du Nord in two days' time at 11.00. and be in their hotel in La Rochelle by 16.00. That would give them plenty of time to plan the search. Elise left him at the Collectionneur and walked around the corner to the Avenue Hoche.

It was nine by the time he got back to his hotel room. He sat on the bed and pulled out his phone. He stared at the device. His mother was eighty years old. He didn't know whether it was a good idea to phone her and rake up the past. In the end, he felt he had no choice. His future and the girl he loved's future hung in the balance. He had to make the call.

He highlighted the number on the screen and pressed the call button. The phone rang.

"Hello".

Gilbert took a deep breath, "Hello, Mum. It's Gilbert."

There was silence, "What do you want, Gilbert?"

He lay back on the bed. This was not the response he had been expecting. His mother could be a cold fish but this was positively freezing, "I'm in France looking for someone and wanted to ask you a few questions?"

There was a huge sigh on the other end of the phone, "Gilbert, I've read the papers and I know what you are trying to do. I don't mind telling you that I am very worried. You may be on a wild goose chase here and end up being very disappointed."

He was immediately defensive, "Why do you say that?"

She snorted, "This girl you are looking for. Who is she? I know what you are like. Even as a child you would fall in love at least ten times per day. What is so special about this girl?"

Gilbert couldn't believe his ears. He decided the best thing to do was just confront her with the evidence, "I think she may be my twin sister."

There was dreadful silence. Eventually, his mother managed a feeble response, "What makes you say that?"

He ploughed ahead, "There has been a campaign on twitter and I met someone this afternoon who knew Margaux when they were about twelve. She had photographs with her. In one of the photographs was a picture of Margaux's father. He is the spitting image of the man you said was my father and who you said died in the Royal Navy."

Again, there was complete quiet on the other end of the phone. After what seemed like an age, his mother did something that Gilbert had never heard her do. In fact, she did something that he had never heard any eighty-year old woman do. She swore hideously.

"The fucking cunts. What a bunch of fucking cunts. If I could get my fucking hands on them, I swear I'd fucking kill them. Good luck in your search, son. When you find out what you need to find out, you can fucking kill them for me because I know you'll fucking want to". She slammed the phone down.

Gilbert was utterly astonished. Where had that come from?

There was a flash of brilliant white light.

She climbed on to the bed beside him. She was in stitches, "I do like your Mum. She doesn't hold back, does she?"

Gilbert grabbed her by the shoulders, "Okay, I thought I'd worked it out but that phone call was the biggest trip to weirdsville I have ever experienced. What on earth is going on?"

She put her finger to his mouth, "Shush. I'm not your twin but we are the same. If you think that the phone call was weird then you had better get ready because you are about to go on the weirdest trip of your life. I mean LSD weird."

Gilbert started chuckling, "Margaux. This is the most fun I've had in years. Let me really enjoy it. Please tell me that you are not in any trouble."

She kissed him, "You are way further forward than even I thought you'd be. I think I can safely say that there is time enough to enjoy it. Just don't linger or dilly dally." There was a flash and she was gone.

Gilbert lay on the bed mulling things over. If Margaux wasn't his twin sister then who was she? Why had his mum reacted in the way she had done over the phone? Why did she refer to fucking cunts instead of fucking cunt? She had definitely used the plural. Who were they? What was the problem?

He got off the bed and changed in to his pyjamas. Tomorrow was another day. He set his alarm for 8.00 and jumped in to bed. As he stared up at the ceiling, he thought about Elise Simon. He was glad she was coming with him to La Rochelle. He liked her. He liked the fact that she had known Margaux when she was younger. It might help.

When the alarm went off in the morning, he jumped out of bed and showered. As he stood in front of the bathroom mirror, he could see the evidence of a poor night's sleep. The reaction from his mother had worried him and he was now worried about her. He would leave things until this afternoon, then he would phone her again. Hopefully, she will have calmed down and be more cogent.

He got dressed in to his blue suit and put on a white shirt and red tie. It would do no harm to evoke the tricolore when he was on French TV. He picked up his diary and checked his schedule. At 11.00, he was meeting Wendy Bouchard from Zone Interdite. They had agreed to do a one off special on the search for Margaux Martin. The programme would be broadcast tonight.

He left his room and wandered downstairs to the restaurant and helped himself to a continental breakfast. He loved a French start to the day. Croissants with hams and cheeses together with a bowl of fruit and a pot of coffee.

At 9.00, precisely, Elise joined him at the table. He poured her a cup of coffee, "I have some news which you may find interesting?"

She took a sip of the dark brown liquid and nodded for him to continue.

"I phoned my mother last night. Margaux is definitely not my twin. Not only that, when I raised the issue she went off in to a tirade and slammed the phone down on me." He explained the rant and the expletives.

Elise was shocked, "I'm astonished. I thought we had worked it out. Why was she so angry?"

Gilbert shrugged, "I'm not sure. I'm going to phone her again, this afternoon and see if I can get more information. Hopefully, she will have calmed down and will want to talk to me."

He looked at his new friend across the table. She was smiling from ear to ear.

"What is making you happy?" he enquired.

She picked up her coffee cup, "I am smiling because this is mystery. There is more to it than we thought originally.

I feel like I am a detective on a case and because I have so much invested in it, myself. It is the best case in the world."

He chuckled, "I'm glad you feel that way. Margaux thinks we are going to discover something weird. I can't help feeling that she is right. I now believe my primary objective is to find this man who appears to be my father. My mother didn't confirm but she didn't deny it either. If I can get to him then I feel that we have a chance of getting to the truth."

Elise looked at him with a serious expression, "I agree with you. Find him and you have the answer. When is your interview?"

He jumped. He'd forgotten about the TV, "It's 11.00. I'm meeting Wendy Bouchard at Metropole on the Avenue Charles de Gaulle."

She held out her hand, "Calm down. I know where it is. It is only a 45-minute walk from here. If we leave at 10.00, we'll be in plenty of time."

He sat down, "I'm glad you're here. I feel a bit jumpy this morning. Something isn't quite right and I can't put my finger on it."

She raised an eyebrow, "Are these your special powers, again?"

He scratched his chin, "Don't underestimate the special powers. I know something isn't quite right and I know I'm missing something that is right in front of me. It's like the car in the photograph. I could see it all along but the significance of it didn't dawn on me immediately.

There is something significant that I'm not seeing. It will come to me."

They finished their coffees and left the hotel for the walk to Metropole TV. They walked down the Rue de Courcelles and joined the Avenue des Ternes.

"You live in a magnificent part of Paris, Madame," he said.

She nodded in agreement, "I was very lucky. My husband was a very rich man. When he died, he left me the apartment on the Avenue Hoche and that was enough to set me up for the rest of my life. I don't really need to work. I just do it to maintain a bit of discipline in my life."

It wasn't long before they turned on to the Avenue Charles de Gaulle. After about 500 metres, the Metropole building heaved in to view. He was disappointed. It looked like a block of flats from the ex-Soviet Union. Gilbert turned to her and smiled, "Here we go".

At reception they asked for Wendy Bouchard. After about five minutes, they were met by a very pleasant blond-haired woman in her late thirties. Gilbert liked her immediately. She had the face of a detective. Just what he needed.

"Monsieur Martin, I'm Wendy Bouchard. How very nice to meet you."

Gilbert stood up and held out his hand, "The pleasure is mine, Madame. This is Elise Simon, she is helping me in my search."

Wendy smiled and nodded at Elise, "Enchanté, Madame".

Elise shook her hand and smiled.

They were bustled through to a well-lit room where a television camera was already waiting. Wendy explained the intended procedure for the interview, "As this is a special programme, we are not doing a studio interview. We are going to conduct the interview in French and edit out any translation difficulties you may have. You can be completely relaxed and ask questions at any time. We'll make sure that the final cut looks good for television."

Gilbert thanked her and sat down, "Do you know the story, Madame?"

She smiled and nodded, "Yes, I've seen the British TV interviews and I've spoken to your agent, Eleanor. I must say, I'm greatly intrigued. It would be good for our audience in France if you could re-cap. It is a great story. I suggest you tell it."

They got themselves settled and Wendy recorded an introductory piece to camera and then she started the interview proper.

"Welcome to France, Mr Martin. Can you explain to our audience what you hope to find out when you are here?"

Gilbert smiled and thanked her, "I'm hoping to find out two things. Firstly, do I have a mental health problem? Am I mad? Secondly, if I'm not mad, why did Margaux Martin follow me home to Scotland in 1983? Who is she? What happened to her and what was it about me that made her follow me home?"

XI

Zone Interdite

Wendy Bouchard smiled, "Let's see if we can help you. Why don't you start at the very beginning and tell us the whole story? Leave nothing out."

Gilbert paused for a second to collect his thoughts, he made himself comfortable in his seat, then he ploughed ahead.

"It all began in La Rochelle on the evening of 28 June 1983. I went to bed excited because I was visiting Châtelaillon-Plage the following day. I dreamt that the next day was going to be wonderfully romantic and that I would meet someone who would change my life forever.

The following day at ten o'clock in the morning I arrived on the beach by coach from La Rochelle, where the school had booked out a hotel for a week.

There are about twenty of us and everybody disappeared in to their little groups. I went off by myself to walk along the shoreline.

I removed my socks and shoes and put them in my rucksack. I started walking along the beach and I let the waves rush over my bare feet. Suddenly, in the white light of the sun, I heard a voice. It was a girl about my age.

"Bonjour," she said.

"Oh, hello".

"Are you English, Monsieur?"

I remember smiling, "No. I'm Scottish, actually. I'm from Edinburgh."

She raised her eyebrows, "Scotland. It is where the monster lives".

I laughed and wiped the sweat from my brow, "Yes, she lives in the loch."

She looked concerned, "You are hot, Monsieur. I will buy you an ice cream if you tell me about this loch."

We walked arm in arm to the ice cream vendor, "What would you like?"

I gave her my best French, "Je voudrais une glace malaga, s'il vous plait, Madame."

She laughed and bought me a rum and raisin ice cream and a vanilla one for herself.

"Now tell me about this loch."

We talked about the loch and she was very interested, "I think I would like to see this loch and the monster."

I licked my ice cream, "Maybe you could come back to Scotland with me and we could go and have a look."

She smiled, "I think I would like that very much."

We sat down on the beach together and she drew out a map on the wet sand, "This is France and this is Scotland. Where is the loch on the map?"

I took my index finger and made a hole in the sand where Inverness is, "Right there"!

She leaned forward and kissed me on the lips. I kissed her back.

She held out her hand, "Come on. Let's take a walk."

We held hands, all the way along Châtelaillon-Plage. At the end of the beach there are rocky pools. We sit down and take a look, "I think Loch Ness is bigger than this," she said laughing.

I laughed too, "Just a bit."

"My name is Margaux Martin. What's yours?"

I must have looked stunned, "My name is Gilbert Martin. We are both the same."

She smiled and looked pleased, "Obviously. I think we are married. Do you want to kiss the bride?"

I leaned forward and opened my mouth just a bit. She grabbed my cheeks and kissed me full on. Her tongue brushed against mine. It was electric.

There was a voice in the distance, "Margaux. Margaux".

She looked at me, "Maman. I must go, for now. I will see you again, Gilbert Martin."

She got up and walked toward the road. She climbed up the sand and just before she left, she looked back and waved. I waved back. She'd gone.

I was about to get on the coach at the end of the afternoon when she rushed up to me, out of nowhere, and pressed a little envelope in my hand, "It is a letter with my address on it. Write to me."

She kissed me on the cheek and hurried away. I looked for her over the heads of all the people. She disappeared over the sand and on to the road. I am sure she looked back, one last time.

It was later that evening, when I was in the bathroom brushing my teeth that she put in her first appearance. I said, "What are you doing here?"

She just smiled, "I'm coming home with you. We are going to see the monster, remember?"

Since that day, she has been with me all of my life. I have never been sure that she is real. I wrote to her at the address she gave me and received no response but she has always been with me.

In the last year, however, things have started to become more urgent. She keeps telling me that they are calling her. I don't know who they are but it appears I have a limited time to find her."

Wendy picked up her notes, "It is an intriguing tale. Do you mind if we go through the theories being discussed, at the moment, on social media? It will help us decide what you need us to help you with."

Gilbert smiled, "By all means. It is a very good idea."

Wendy nodded, "Let's take the mental health issue first. How do you know that you are not mad?"

Gilbert stopped for a second, "Other people have felt her presence and other people have heard her speak. These are professionals with good credentials. I can safely say that I am not mad but understand if certain others wish to believe that I am. Seeing is believing, I suppose."

Wendy chuckled, "Indeed, it is. I have spoken to your agent who can corroborate that a room full of people heard Margaux in London. Do you think she is a ghost?"

Again, he paused so that the viewers could see he was thinking about his answers carefully, "I no longer believe her to be a ghost. She has asked us to find her and that suggests that she is a corporeal entity."

Wendy put her notes down on the floor, "How do we find her?"

Gilbert sat up in his seat, "I think we find her father. Yesterday, I met with Elise Simon, who was Margaux's childhood friend. She gave me this photograph of Margaux's father yesterday." He handed over the restaurant photograph.

"This was taken in a restaurant in Bordeaux called Le Chapon Fin on July 21st 1983. When I saw the photograph, it gave me terrible goose bumps. Margaux's father is the spitting image of my own late father. Apparently, he died when I was about two years old and yet here is his doppelganger in a restaurant in Bordeaux, ten years later."

Wendy suddenly sat up and came alive, "Are you saying that this is your father?"

Gilbert nodded, "Yes, I believe this is my father. I phoned my mother to question her last night but she became terribly agitated. She did not deny that this man was my father."

Wendy put two and two together, "Then, surely, Margaux is your sister?"

Gilbert shrugged, "She says we are the same but we are not twins. If we are not twins, then we can't be brother and sister as we are the same age."

Wendy frowned. She really looked like she should have her own detective agency, "Could you be clones?"

Gilbert sat stunned. The thought had not occurred to him, "I've no idea. I need to find her father. If I can do that then maybe I'll get some answers and get closer to the truth."

Wendy nodded, "What do you know about him?"

Gilbert sighed, "Not that much really. I know that his name is Monsieur Martin. He lived in Margaux in 1983 on the Avenue Jeanne D'Arc. He had a daughter called Margaux born in 1970 and that he drove a brown Citroen DS. That is all I know for certain. If he is, indeed, my father, then his name is Robert and he was married to my mother, whose name is Margaret."

Wendy smiled, "It may be enough, Monsieur. How do our viewers contact you?"

"Your viewers can contact my agent by tweeting using the hashtag #findme or alternatively, they can request an e mail address using the same hashtag." He looked directly at the camera, "I would be grateful for any help you can give me. This has become urgent now and I need to find Margaux soon."

Madame Bouchard looked at him seriously, "What are your next steps?"

He scratched his chin, "I'm travelling down to La Rochelle with Madame Simon tomorrow and from there, we are heading down to the Haut-Medoc. There is no reasonable lead that we will not look at and follow through on.

It had always been my belief that she is in France and because she came from Gironde, my expectation is that she will be found there. I cannot tell you why I feel that this is true it's just a sixth sense that I have."

Wendy chuckled, "Do not worry about that Monsieur. There is so much mystery surrounding this case that a bit of sixth sense is quite believable. Gilbert Martin, thank you very much for coming in and sharing your story. It has been a great pleasure and if our viewers can help then I am sure that they will."

She turned to the camera and gave her closing piece.

When they were finished, Gilbert stood up and thanked her, "I think that went rather well."

Madame Bouchard nodded, "Yes. I thought you were very good. It is a great story. Let us take copies of the photographs and we will broadcast them tonight together with the contact details."

Twenty minutes later, Gilbert and Elise were back on the Avenue Charles de Gaulle, "What now?" asked Elise.

Gilbert pursed his lips, "Why don't we take a walk to Gare du Nord. I can buy your train tickets to La Rochelle and then I will buy you lunch at Etoile du Nord. I think it is run by Thierry Marx."

Elise laughed happily, "I think I like working with you, Gilbert. Lunch breaks are exceptional."

He raised a finger in a moralistic sort of way, "Never underestimate the importance of a meal. It is not just a means of replenishing the body. You should always endeavour to replenish the soul."

She nodded enthusiastically, "I heartily agree."

They walked back to Courcelles. When they crossed over the Avenue Hoche, Elise pointed to her apartment. It was above a Brasserie called La Belle Poule, which he knew well. It looked expensive. Gilbert loved the eighth arrondissement. It was classy. If he ever bought an apartment in Paris, it would be here. They headed down Haussmann and joined the Rue de la Pepiniere and then on to Saint-Lazare. Eventually, they came to Gare du Nord.

"I'm starving." announced Elise.

Gilbert smiled, "Me too. It is the walking. It builds up a great appetite."

He bought the tickets and went straight to the restaurant. When they were seated, he looked around, "I think there is only one city in the world that would think of putting a Michelin starred chef in a train station restaurant."

Elise agreed, "Only in Paris, Monsieur."

They both ordered the honey battered fish and chips. When they came, Elise looked curiously at her platter, "Do you eat these regularly in England?"

He couldn't help but laugh, "Don't worry. They taste a lot better than they look."

It didn't take her long to demolish the platter. When she put her knife and fork on the plate, she conceded that they had been very good.

Gilbert looked at her seriously, "When we come back here tomorrow, it will be day one in the search for Margaux Martin. My expectation is that we will put our heart and soul in to it and not stop until we have uncovered the truth."

She returned his extremely serious look, "I hear you, Monsieur."

XII

La Rochelle

The eleven o'clock train from Gare du Nord to La Rochelle left exactly on time.

Gilbert felt like a horse waiting in the paddock. He just wanted the starting pistol to go off so that he could jump the first fence. Elise leaned across the table and put her hand over his, "Relax. This is the TGV. Once the train leaves the station, we'll be off like the wind."

It was true. The Train a Grande Vitesse was a miracle of modern engineering. It went like a bullet. When they were out in the open countryside, the world whizzed past.

He ordered two coffees from the trolley, "I've been thinking. How do you feel about conducting a review of social media content when we get to La Rochelle? Eleanor has agreed to vet out all the nonsense and only send me the viable leads by e mail. We could spend today prioritising them in to a list. Hopefully, there won't be that many."

Elise sipped her coffee, "I think that is a great idea. It might be worthwhile to group the leads in to regions. If we centre our search on the village of Margaux itself, we could branch out from there."

Gilbert nodded, "Yes, I like the sound of that. Do you think we should look for accommodation in Bordeaux or should we return to La Rochelle each night?"

She thought about it, "Let's play it by ear. We could use La Rochelle as a base, leave our luggage there and travel light. We could decide what to do each day. You never know, we may end up going a bit further afield."

There was a ping on his mobile phone to notify him that he'd just received a text. He pulled out the device and put his finger on the green button, "It's Eleanor. My book is going to number one in the bestseller charts tomorrow. The sales in the first week are over 100,000."

Elise opened her eyes wide, "That's good, isn't it?"

He chuckled, "It's better than good. If you exceed 30,000 in the first week you can just about guarantee a classic novel. This is more than three times that. I might be able to buy my apartment in Paris after all."

Her face lit up, "We could be neighbours. You like the eighth arrondissement, do you not?"

He smiled, "Yes, that would be my first choice. If I make really big money then I'll be on the Boulevard Haussmann. Not only will I be your neighbour, I'll be able to look down on you from my ivory tower."

She let out a brilliantly happy laugh, "I don't think you're the type to look down on anyone."

He made a face, "I don't know about that. Coming from Edinburgh, I've always looked down on Scottish people from other cities. Glaswegians, Dundonians, Aberdonians and even Stirlingers, who think they are a cut above the rest of us but aren't really."

She looked at him curiously, "What are Dundonians like?"

He laughed, "Now you're talking. They are Scots with a very strange and mysterious accent. History tells us that they are addicted to something called a "peh". It is a double-crust pastry filled with spiced and minced mutton. It is usually served with baked beans and Houses of Parliament sauce."

She screwed her face up, "That sounds revolting. What is Houses of Parliament sauce?"

He scratched his head, "It is usually referred to as HP sauce and is made from spiced molasses and vinegar."

Elise put her chin on her hand and stared at him, "Seriously. Scottish people have the most ridiculous cuisine I have ever heard of. Haggis, peh and now HP sauce. What next? Deep fried chocolate?"

Gilbert looked down at his coffee, "Er. I'm rather afraid we've been there, too."

She wasn't done, "Tell me about Aberdonians. What are they like?"

He took a sip of his drink, "Well, they are a real mystery. They don't just have a funny accent, they have a completely different language. Men are called "loons" and women are called "quines". They eat something called a "rowie" which is basically a croissant with a death wish. There is enough butter in a single "rowie" to bake a cake."

"Glaswegians?"

He sighed, "They are known as death eaters. Imagine the unhealthiest cuisine in the universe and then wrap a kebab round it and deep fry it. They eat chips with everything. A Glasgow salad is effectively a plate of chips.

There was a famous court case in Glasgow where a man was accused of eating a tomato. He was hanged for sorcery."

Elise looked at him with a dead pan face, "Okay, so you do look down on people. I'm from Gironde, not from Paris, would you really look down on me?"

He smiled at her, "Not really. France has a better class of peasant than most other countries. You don't find them eating chips, they prefer a higher standard of lunch. Fruit, seafood, pâtés, fromages and excellent boulangerie. There is really very little to look down upon."

She sat back in her seat with a wry smile, "I'm glad to hear it, Monsieur."

The train arrived in La Rochelle at a quarter to three. They collected their luggage and headed for the taxi rank, "I've booked us in to the same hotel I stayed in 1983."

Elise raised an eyebrow, "Somehow, I'm not surprised."

They were ten minutes in the taxi through the centre of town. When the cab pulled up at the hotel, Gilbert felt all the memories come rushing back to him.

The Hotel Saint-Nicolas was situated between the Quai Maubec and the Quai Valin. It was constructed from stone that shone pale yellow in the sunshine. Gilbert remembered the large arch windows at the front of the building that looked on to a patio where guests could enjoy a drink in the afternoon sun. He felt he was coming home.

They checked in to their rooms and were seated at a table on the terrace within twenty minutes, "Would you like a drink?" asked Gilbert.

Elise breathed out, "Oh, yes please. A glass of Chablis would go down very well at this moment in time."

Gilbert ordered two glasses of Chablis from the waiter. He opened his iPad, "Right. Let's see what e-mails, we have from Eleanor."

Elise pulled out her notebook and sat with a pen at the ready.

Gilbert opened his e-mail account and looked at the e-mails sent from his agent. She had vetted out all the nonsense and had only included the responses that she felt were genuine leads. She had headed up each e-mail with the region of interest. There were twenty-four e-mails in total.

Gilbert cleared his throat, "We have twenty-four e-mails in total and three of those are centred on Margaux itself. We have four in Pessac and seventeen in the greater Bordeaux region."

Elise frowned, "Check the Margaux ones first. See what they are saying."

He opened the first e-mail, "From Veronique Ségur. I live

on the Avenue Jeanne D'Arc. Robert and Elizabeth Martin lived next door to me until 1983 when they left without warning overnight. They had a daughter called Margaux who was hurt in a car accident. That is all I remember."

Elise sipped her wine, "That is encouraging. If Margaux's stepmother was called Elizabeth then that could be them."

Gilbert nodded, "It's them. I know Martin is a common surname in France but when they have a daughter called Margaux hurt in a car accident, then you have to believe it's them."

He opened the second Margaux e-mail, "From Pierre Dubois. In 1983, I worked for Chateau Margaux with a Robert Martin who was the vigneron. I was the cellar manager. With no warning, he moved to Pessac in the summer of 1983. One minute he was there, the next he was gone."

They both looked at each other. It was Elise who broke the silence, "Could Margaux's father have been the vintner at Chateau Margaux?"

Gilbert's eyes opened wide, "What if he felt he had to leave in a hurry and get another job. Pessac would be a definite possibility."

Elise looked a bit dubious, "You don't think he went from Margaux to Haut-Brion just like that?"

Gilbert shrugged, "Why not? One premier cru to another. It makes sense to me."

He opened the third e-mail, "My name is Charlotte Durand. I knew an Elizabeth Martin from Margaux in 1983. She had a daughter called Margaux who was hurt in a car accident in La Rochelle. I was a nurse at the Hospital St Nicolas de Blaye. The child was moved to the Hospital Pellegrin in Bordeaux and I know that the family moved there to be with the daughter."

Gilbert whistled, "That has got to be our Margaux."

Elise nodded, "No doubt. These are great leads. I think we

should start chasing these down first thing tomorrow. Let's check out the Pessac e-mails. If Monsieur Martin moved to Pessac to be with Margaux then he may still be there."

He opened the first Pessac e-mail, "My name is Jean-Phillippe Delmas, I am the manager of Chateau Haut-Brion. My father, Jean-Bernard, who was manager before me, employed a Robert Martin as vintner between 1983 and 1995 when he retired aged 60.

My understanding is that M Martin had a daughter who was ill and he cared for her in Pessac. Her name was Margaux."

Elise let out an explosive breath, "Well, I'll be damned."

Gilbert chuckled, "What were you saying about moving to Haut-Brion, just like that?"

She laughed, "There must be more to it than that. Remember, it is not unusual for Vintners to be freelance here in Bordeaux. He could have already worked for them in the past and then made it a more permanent arrangement."

Gilbert nodded his head, "Yes. I think you are right. He will have been known to them and they may have hired him on a permanent basis as a result of the issue with Margaux."

Elise looked excited and busy scribbling away, "Open the next one."

He clicked on the next e-mail, "Hello. My name is Bertrand Moreau. I work at the Aéroport de Bordeaux. In 1997, I moved from Pessac to Merignac to be closer to my job. In Pessac, my old neighbour was a Robert Martin who had a sick daughter called Margaux.

There was no woman living with him at the time but I believe the child's mother was called Elisabeth. I lived on the Rue de Poilus in Pessac."

Gilbert sat back in his chair, "I think Eleanor has done a great job. I feel we are getting closer to finding the father. Every lead is dynamite."

Elise agreed, "Okay. We know where he was in 1997. He'd just retired from his job and was living in Pessac. That was still twenty-one years ago."

Gilbert sighed, "You are right. We need something more up to date."

He was about to click on the next e-mail, when his mobile started to ring. He looked at the screen. It was Eleanor, "I'd better answer. It's Eleanor."

He swiped the screen and placed the device at his ear, "Hello."

There was a pause, "Gilbert. It's Eleanor. I'm afraid I'm going to have to ask you to sit down. I have some bad news."

He felt the hairs at his neck stand on end and his skin started to crawl, "I'm sitting. What is it?"

She breathed out, "Oh, Gilbert, I'm so sorry but I've had Police Scotland on the phone. I'm afraid it's your mother. She's dead.

She was found by a neighbour yesterday morning. She was lying in the hallway with the phone lying on the floor. The police have checked the phone records. It seems you were the last person she spoke to."

XIII

Disaster & Dreams

Gilbert stared in to space. He couldn't speak. He couldn't move.

"What is it?" asked Elise.

He looked in her direction, "It's my mother. She's dead."

Elise put her hand to her mouth, "Oh, my God."

Gilbert took a sip of his wine, "Eleanor. I'm sorry. I need a bit of time to think. Can I phone you back?"

She sounded sympathetic, "Of course, Gilbert. Phone me back when you can."

Gilbert pressed the red button on the phone and killed the call. He looked at Elise, "Apparently, I was the last person to speak to her. She was found in the hallway with the phone on the floor."

Elise looked horrified, "You don't think your phone call had anything to do with it?"

He gazed at her flatly, "I think we both know that it did. The funny thing is, I feel nothing really. My mother was a cold fish at the best of times and now that I know that she was hiding something from me, I don't feel as if I actually knew who she was."

Elise put her hand on his, "I know how you feel. In situations like this, we are supposed to be distraught but often we just don't feel that way."

Gilbert suddenly looked annoyed, "I can't go home now. Margaux has asked us to find her urgently. If I go home for the funeral, then I delay the search for at least a week. I need an excuse to delay things so that I can stay here and continue looking for Margaux."

Elise thought about it, "Just tell your agent that. She's obviously on your side and I think she'll understand. If you tell her to find a way to delay your return, she'll come up with something."

Gilbert knew that she was right. Eleanor would find a way and she was too caught up in the whole business to allow anything to deter Gilbert from finding out the truth. He decided to call her straight back.

"Eleanor. It's Gilbert. I know this is going to sound awfully heartless but I need to stay in France to find Margaux. The leads you gave us are dynamite and we want to start chasing them down tomorrow.

Margaux says that she is running out of time and we need to find her urgently. If I come home for the funeral then I lose out on a week and I don't think I can afford to do that. I need you to find me an excuse not to return to the UK."

There was silence. Eventually she said, "I understand, completely. Leave it to me. I'll think of something and I'll phone you back."

Gilbert put his mobile back on the table. He looked at Elise, "She'll think of something. I think we have one week to find Margaux. If I don't find her in that time, I'll have to go back to Britain without her. I can only stay for so long."

Elise nodded, "Yes, I know. One week. I think that's all we need. You stay here and finish the e-mails. I'm going off to hire a car so that we can leave from here first thing in the morning. I'll meet you back her for dinner at say eight?"

"Eight o'clock. See you then."

As Elise walked off, Gilbert sat back in his chair. He was sorry that his mother had passed away but the truth was he didn't feel anything. He had moved to London to get away from her and so that he could be alone with Margaux. His mum didn't do imaginary friends, in fact, his mum didn't do friends.

However, he knew that it would look dreadful if he didn't return soon. He hoped Eleanor could come up with a good cover story.

He went through the rest of the Pessac e-mails. They were more or less the same as the last one. The trail went cold in 1999, when Robert Martin appeared to move from his house in Pessac to God knows where. There was one lead for Elizabeth Martin in St Genes, Bordeaux. Gilbert took a note of that. It was near the hospital so it was a definite possibility.

At six o'clock, he returned to his room to shower and get ready for dinner. There was something nagging at him and he couldn't quite put his finger on it. He knew it was something to do with Elizabeth Martin but the penny would not drop.

He had experienced these situations before and he knew that the wrong thing to do was push it. It was almost as if his subconscious worked on the problem and when it had the answer, it would let him know. It was like the cryptic crossword in The Guardian. He would go to bed with an unanswered clue that he had no idea how to solve and then he would awake the next morning with the answer.

At eight, he went down to join Elise for dinner. She had already secured a table and was waiting for him, "How did you get on?" he enquired.

She smiled, "I've hired a nice big Audi A4 for our trip to Margaux. I love driving but don't get much of a chance in Paris. The roads are full of mad men. It is quite different down here so I thought I'd treat us to a comfortable ride."

He was pleased, "Thank you, Elise. That's a weight off my mind".

She picked up the menu, "What about you? Were there any other interesting e-mails?"

He pursed his lips, "The trail for Robert Martin goes cold in 1999. He apparently moved from Pessac at that time and I don't have any other leads as yet. We do, however, have a lead for Elizabeth. She may be living in the quartier, St Genes in Bordeaux."

Elise raised her eyebrows, "That's near the hospital. I bet that's where she is now."

Suddenly, Gilbert felt that shock when he put two and two together. He knew that Elise was talking about Elizabeth but what if Margaux, herself, was still at the hospital?

Elise leaned forward, "What is it? You look like you have seen a ghost."

Gilbert could barely contain his excitement, "What if Margaux is still at the hospital? What if she never left there? What if she is in a long-term coma and nobody has pulled the plug?"

Elise face transformed, "Let's make that our priority. Let's go to the hospital first and see what we can find out."

Dinner was slightly disappointing but only because they had dined so well in Paris. They had lobster bisque followed by a gourmet burger. Elise had suggested that they forego the wine on account of their mission the following morning. Gilbert reluctantly agreed.

As they were finishing their coffee, Gilbert's mobile rang again. It was Eleanor, "I have something. I'm afraid it isn't much but it is the best I can come up with.

If Police Scotland get back in touch, I'm going to tell them I have been unable to contact you by mobile. If the worst comes to the worst, just say that you forgot to bring your charger with you and that your phone ran out of juice."

Gilbert hesitated, "It's not much but I think it will do. It buys us a couple of days at least. The leads you have given us have been very good indeed. I'll call you tomorrow and let you know how we've done."

She sounded optimistic, "Stick at it. If your close, you never know. You might have this sown up by the end of the week. Good luck."

He put the phone down and turned to Elise, "Eleanor suggests that I say I forgot my phone charger and I ran out of battery."

She shrugged, "It will do. I'm going to bed. Let's meet down here at seven in the morning. We'll be on the road by seven-thirty and in Bordeaux by nine-thirty."

When Gilbert got back to his room, he realised that he was exhausted. He changed in to his pyjamas and jumped in to bed. He turned out the lamp and was asleep almost before the light faded.

He found himself in darkness. In the background he could hear the familiar guitar introduction of one of his favourite songs from his teenage years. It was a song he had played for Margaux when she first arrived in Scotland with him.

Suddenly, there was a brilliant flash of white light and she was there at his side, holding his hand.

To the centre of the city where all roads meet
Waiting for you
To the depths of the ocean where all hopes sank
Searching for you
I was moving through the silence without motion
Waiting for you
In a room with a window in the corner
I found truth

In the shadowplay, acting out your own death
Knowing no more
As the assassins all grouped in four lines
Dancing on the floor
And with cold steel, odour on their bodies

Made a move to connect
But I could only stare in disbelief
As the crowds all left

As the song moved in to its outro, she smiled at him, "I'm sorry about your mother."

He bent down and lifted her in to his arms, "There's no need to be. She was always a bit distant. I've got everything I need right here. I always have, ever since I was thirteen."

She looked pleased, "I am so glad to hear you say that and I'm glad that you have decided to stay and look for me. I think you are very close now. Follow the leads you have and you will find my father."

He looked at her with surprise, "The trail for your father goes cold after 1999. He seems to have moved from Pessac at that point."

She nodded her head, "Yes, he moved from Pessac at that point but the trail is hot. You have already received an e-mail from someone who can tell you where he is now. It is just that it is against the law to provide you with this information."

Gilbert frowned, "Can you tell me more."

She shook her head, "Just think and use your head, ma Chérie. It is all in there you know". She tapped his temple.

Gilbert wasn't sure whether to ask his next question. In the end, he felt he had no choice, "Is your father, my father?"

She stared at him, "In truth, I'm not sure. You are about to uncover the disaster. I want you to remember this. It was meant to be a bit of fun. Something went wrong and it got horribly complicated. In the end, everybody got hurt. I need you to be my Gilbert. Forgive as I have forgiven.

When I was young, I found out about it and forced my father to tell me the truth. Even he wasn't totally sure what happened. All I know is that I dreamed of meeting you. Imagine my surprise when you turned up on our beach. Once I met you, I could never leave you.

If you get this right, it will be your turn for the dream to come true. We will be there again. In the twilight. On Châtelaillon-Plage."

The light suddenly increased and she was gone. He woke with a start. There was a knocking on his door. He got up and turned on the light. When he opened the door, it was Elise, "Something has been bothering me and it just came to me. I needed to tell you, in case I forgot."

He stood aside and let her in to the room, "What is it?"

She was excited, "If Robert Martin retired from Haut-Brion, then the likelihood is that they will be paying his pension. If they are paying his pension then surely, they will have his up to date address."

She'd got it. He danced a jig.

XIV

Médoc

At eight thirty, the following morning, Elise Simon was at the wheel of the hired Audi heading down the A10 towards Bordeaux. For a Friday morning, the road was exceptionally quiet.

"Where is all the traffic?" asked Gilbert.

Elise shrugged, "I think it is because it is Good Friday. I don't know how it is in England but a lot of people, in France, still observe the holiday and still actually go to church."

Gilbert had forgotten about Easter. It was a favourite time of year for Margaux. He remembered, when they were younger, saving the best of his Easter eggs for her. She liked the Lindt ones which she referred to as the "good chocolate".

He turned on the radio. They were playing the Good Friday music from Wagner's Parsifal. How very appropriate. He turned to Elise, "I have a very good feeling about today."

She chuckled, "So, do I, Monsieur. So, do I. Easter is a time for re-birth. You have always thought that the fates were following you. Perhaps it wasn't the fates. Perhaps it was something much more powerful."

He smiled. Something much more powerful. He wasn't a religious person but he had always admired Jesus and his message of peace and love. It wouldn't bother him at all if He was responsible. In fact, the more he thought about it, the more he liked the idea.

At nine-thirty, they pulled into the car park at the Hospital

Pellegrin on the outskirts of Bordeaux. Gilbert put a few euros in the ticket machine and stuck the pass to the windscreen, "We have an hour, that should be plenty of time."

Together, they walked to the main reception. As they approached Gilbert suggested that she do the talking and just ask if there was a patient called Margaux Martin in the hospital.

Elise walked up to the main desk. A very pleasant, middle-aged, woman asked if she could help.

"Do you have a patient called Margaux Martin in the hospital?" enquired Elise.

The woman looked surprised and then her gaze rested on Gilbert. Her eyes widened, "Zone Interdite. I saw the Programme on television. She is definitely not here but everybody has been talking about it. Our records only go back six years, I'm afraid."

Elise hesitated, "Does no-one remember the case?"

The woman made a face, "It is such a long time ago. Most of the people who worked here have retired by now. It has been thirty-five years."

Gilbert's heart sank. He should have expected this but a small part of him had been hoping that she would still be here.

The woman noted Gilbert's disappointment and turned to Elise, "Give me your mobile phone number. I will make enquiries and see if we can find out something for you."

Elise gave the woman her mobile number and they both returned to the car. Gilbert got in the passenger seat and let his shoulders slump, "Well, that was a waste of time."

Elise' however, had a different point of view, "It wasn't a waste of time. We know for definite she is not here. We have made an ally who is now making enquiries on our behalf. Do not be discouraged, Monsieur. We are following a trail that is thirty-five years old. Nobody said it was going to be easy."

Gilbert sighed, "You are right. Where next?"

Elise had already started the car, "Chateau Haut-Brion. I phoned earlier this morning and advised them to let Monsieur Delmas know that we would drop by this morning. He is the manager and the one who sent the e-mail."

Gilbert brightened, "The pension. I hope your powers of persuasion are good".

She sniffed, "I don't think they need to be. He wants to help, otherwise he wouldn't have sent the e-mail in the first place."

They were less than ten minutes in the car when Elise turned in to a beautifully gate-posted mansion. Gilbert thought the house looked Georgian and reminded him a little bit of Edinburgh. The stone looked familiar.

They parked the car and made their way to reception. A young woman attended to them and when Elise mentioned that she had phoned ahead earlier that morning the woman smiled, "Monsieur Delmas is expecting you. Please wait. He'll be a few minutes."

After about five minutes the young woman approached and asked them to follow her. She led them to a large ground floor office where a smartly dressed old man was seated at a desk, "Monsieur Martin, Ms Simon, please come in and take a seat". He stood and shook their hands, "What can I do for you?"

Jean-Phillipe Delmas looked like a kindly man and it gave Gilbert the hope and encouragement that he needed, "Monsieur Delmas. Firstly, thank you for seeing us. As you sent the e-mail, I'm assuming that you are acquainted with our situation and that you have seen the television programme that was aired the other night?"

Monsieur Delmas nodded, "Yes. It is mysterious case. If I can help in any way, I will."

Gilbert looked at Elise and she nodded almost imperceptibly, "It is our belief that the Robert Martin you mentioned in your e-mail is indeed the father of our Margaux.

Unfortunately, we have been unable to locate him. The trail goes cold in 1999, when he apparently moved from Pessac. However, if he retired from Haut-Brion, we had the idea that you may be paying him a pension. If you are paying him a pension, then you will have his up to date address."

Monsieur Delmas looked at them both and smiled, "I can see that we are all of a similar mind, Monsieur.

You know, of course, that it would be against the law for me to divulge the personal information of a former employee and we take every reasonable precaution to protect that information.

However, there is nothing I can do about people who snoop around and pry in to other people's business. If, for example, I was to leave a note unattended on my desk and I turned around to look out the window, there is nothing I could reasonably do to prevent these people from taking a note of the contents of that piece of paper."

He nodded at the desk and turned around to look out of the window.

Elise pulled out her notebook and pen. They both leaned forward and looked at the note.

M R Martin
4 Rue Jules Verne
33250 Pauillac

Elise scribbled down the address and closed her notebook.

Monsieur Delmas turned around. He looked directly at Gilbert, "Listen to me. You were not here and you have not spoken to me.

Your father is an old friend. The address I have just given you is the family home. It was his mother's house. It is where he was born and where, I believe, you were born too, Gilbert. Pauillac is the village of your birth."

Gilbert couldn't move. He was stunned, "How do you know that?"

Monsieur Delmas chuckled, "We have met before, my boy. Just after you were born. I remember you very well. As I have said already, Robert is an old friend.

I would consider it a great favour if you could resolve this mess. Put it to bed, once and for all."

Gilbert felt his skin go clammy, "I take it you know what happened?"

Monsieur Delmas face transformed. He looked like a man who was about to shed tears, "Of course, I know but it is not for me to say. It is for your father to tell the story. May I give you a bit of advice?"

Gilbert nodded. He couldn't speak.

The old man sat down, "You will be angry when you hear the tale. Trust me, there is no point.

As a cold-blooded outsider who looked in at the scene, at the time, I can assure you that no-one was to blame. It is a tragedy. A hideous little tragedy that had far reaching repercussions. Please be strong, son and remember that blame has no authority. Only love and forgiveness have authority. They have the authority of kindness."

Gilbert felt very emotional. He stood up and held out his hand, "Monsieur Delmas, I don't know how to thank you. I will remember your words and I promise to be strong."

The old man nodded and shook his hand, "If it is any help, I want you to know that your father had no choice about what happened to you. Your mother was a very difficult person to deal with. I take it she knows you are here?"

Gilbert couldn't help smiling, "She died two days ago."

Monsieur Delmas eyes opened wide and he burst out laughing, "Of course, she did. How very fitting."

Gilbert started to laugh, "I can't help but agree with you."

The old man nodded, "That's the spirit, Gilbert. I have a

very good feeling about this at last."

Gilbert and Elise said their goodbyes and returned to the car. When they were inside, they looked at each other. Gilbert spoke first, "I think we've found him. I can feel it. You said that a higher power was willing us on. I'm prepared to believe that utterly now. I can almost touch her."

Elise was smiling and he could see that she agreed with him, "Yes. I feel it too. We are close. Remember what Monsieur Delmas said. I suspect that you are going to find out something terrible. Please prepare yourself for the worst, Gilbert. Hope for the best."

He made a solemn face to show that he took her warning seriously, "In the hope of preparing for the best, do you think we have time to stop by a shop? I have this overwhelming desire to buy something that I think I'm going to need. Please don't ask too many questions. It is just a feeling I have."

She looked at him curiously, "Special powers, again? We have all the time in the world. Where would you like me to take you?"

He grinned, "Un Chocolatier, s'il vous plait."

She started to laugh, "I think I know where we are going with this". She checked her sat-nav and found a Leonidas just five minutes away on the Avenue Pasteur, "Is that okay? It is Belgian chocolate. I know them from Paris, they are very good."

Gilbert sat back in the passenger seat, "Leonidas will do perfectly."

When they arrived at the shop, they were able to park the car just outside on the kerb. Gilbert had a very good feeling about the place. The shop had a traditional blue canopy and the window screamed "artisan". He needed something special.

They jumped out of the car and went inside, "What are

you looking for?" enquired Elise.

Gilbert shrugged, "I'll know it when I see it."

And then he did see it. It was in a display all by itself. It was simple and it looked expensive. It was perfect.

He turned to the shopkeeper, "How much is that, Monsieur?"

The shopkeeper looked apologetic, "I'm afraid it is 100 euros, Monsieur."

Gilbert couldn't believe his luck, "I'll take it."

The shopkeeper looked at him like he was crazy but he collected the item and wrapped it for him. Gilbert paid him the money. When they were back in the car he noted that Elise had a tear in her eye, "I think she will love it," she said.

Gilbert fastened his seat belt, "Pauillac, Madame. Rue Jules Verne."

She revved the engine, "Certainly, Monsieur. Pauillac."

They were on the A630 almost immediately. After five minutes, Gilbert commented, "It is fitting that our voyages extraordinaires should end at the Rue Jules Verne, don't you think?"

Elise Simon laughed, "There is nothing about this journey that surprises me anymore. I am a firm believer in the supernatural. When this is all over. I think I might write a book."

XV

Place de Naissance

Elise passed the ramp for the D1215 and the road to Pauillac, "What are you doing?" Asked Gilbert.

She chuckled, "You are forgetting, Monsieur, that I come from here. If I stay on this road, we pass through Margaux and my home village of Cantanac. I thought you might like to see where we grew up. It will soon be lunchtime. We could stop for a bite in Margaux, if you like?"

Gilbert relaxed, "That is a great idea. Lunch on me in Margaux."

Elise started to giggle, "I'm so sorry, Monsieur. I feel like a leech. You are just about to buy me lunch in another Michelin starred restaurant. Le Savoie in Margaux is famous and the wine list is out of this world."

Gilbert just laughed. He couldn't believe his luck, "I'm coming home, Elise. This my place de naissance, too. The stars are aligned and the prodigal son returns. I hope it costs me an absolute fortune."

Elise drove for another half hour before she pulled in to the village of Margaux, "It is one o'clock now. Your father will also be having lunch. Let's have our meal and make a plan. We can aim to arrive at Pauillac for two-thirty."

Restaurant Le Savoie was a two-storey stone building with a colonnade at the entrance. Gilbert was reminded a little bit of a roman villa. There was a patio at the front where several patrons were enjoying a glass of wine.

The inside of the building was very bright with whitewashed walls everywhere. The maître kissed Elise on both cheeks and gave her a hug. He showed them to a table overlooking the restaurant.

"An old friend?" enquired Gilbert

She smiled, "Yes, we were at school together. Don't worry about a thing. I know everybody here."

Elise ordered salmon and caviar followed by veal. Gilbert went for the lamprey followed by beef, "Should we order a bottle of wine?"

Elise suggested a compromise, "Let's have one glass each. I've got the car, remember."

They each ordered a glass of Chateau Margaux.

Gilbert sat back in his seat, "What do you think the plan should be?"

Elise shrugged, "I think we knock on the door, introduce ourselves and let your father do the talking. I think he'll want to talk. I remember him as a very nice man and I think he'll want to tell you the truth and get everything off his chest.

Once he has done that then hopefully we can persuade him to take us to see Margaux, wherever she is."

Gilbert sipped his wine, "Where do you think she'll be?"

Elise's face assumed a pensive expression, "I think she will be close by. It is fairly certain that she is in a coma from the accident in 1983. I'm expecting her to be in a private nursing home."

Gilbert nodded, "That is my thought, also. How far away are we from Pauillac?"

Elise pursed her lips, "We're about half an hour away by car. Look, I know you are nervous but we are right where we need to be. My advice is to relax and enjoy your lunch."

Gilbert breathed out, "I'm sorry. I'm getting anxious because I know I can't hang around forever. If Mum hadn't popped her clogs, it would be a different story but the reality is I must return for the funeral at some point."

Elise looked sympathetic to show that she understood, "The British are a strange race with your figures of speech. How can you refer to your Mum "popping her clogs"? I take it that means she is dead?"

Gilbert started laughing, "Don't worry, you'll get used to it. We have a number of euphemisms for death. Popping your clogs is just one of them."

She shook her head, "Unbelievable. What are the others"?

He scratched his chin, "Let me see. There is "kicking the bucket", "buying the farm", "biting the dust", "shuffling off one's mortal coil", "meeting one's maker", "cashing in one's chips", "going belly up", "ceasing to exist", "passing away", "giving up the ghost", "breathing one's last", "expiring", "going the way of all flesh", "meeting one's sad demise", "conking" and "passing over to the other side"."

Elise was in stitches, "Good grief. Do the British have a fascination with death?"

Gilbert shrugged, "No. We have Monty Python and a dead parrot. There is no more to it than that."

She looked a bit perplexed "Why buying the farm? What has that to do with dying?"

He raised his eyebrows, "You know. I really have no idea at all."

The waiter came over with their starters. They were both famished and tucked in straight away.

Gilbert chewed his lamprey, "I can see why this is a Michelin starred restaurant."

Elise was delighted, "I was hoping you would like it. I think you are going to love this region of France. It is your birthplace after all but you have the temperament for it. You enjoy good food and good wine. There is nowhere better. I don't think Paris has a better carte des vins."

He couldn't help but agree. He had not seen a menu with

as many premier crus in his life.

When the meal was over, they sat drinking coffee and eating little squares of chocolate. Gilbert mentally prepared himself for what lay ahead, "Do you think he will be surprised to see us?"

Elise thought about it as she sipped her coffee, "No. I think he is waiting for you. I think he will be expecting you."

This caused Gilbert a slight concern, "Why didn't he write to us?"

She smiled, "You'll have to ask him that but I've been sitting here wondering myself. I can only suggest that it has something to do with the difficulty Monsieur Delmas mentioned."

Gilbert thought she might be right. He checked his watch and downed the last dregs of his coffee, "Ready?"

She smiled, "Ready when you are."

He paid the bill and they wandered out to the car. They got in and fastened their seatbelts. Elise started the engine and they took the road north to Pauillac.

As they left Margaux, Gilbert got the uneasy feeling that he was leaving behind something familiar. It seemed that every road they went down and every corner they turned was known to him in some way.

He asked the question that had been nagging at him for a while "Do you have family, who still lives here?"

Elise nodded, "Yes. My parents are still alive and live in Cantanac. We can drop in on them later. If we need a place to stay, they'll happily put us up."

They passed through Cantanac and Gilbert felt that they were truly in rural France. The villages were not dissimilar to the ones found in the highlands of Scotland. People made a living here and they didn't always have the money to splash out on niceties. The villages felt as if someone was living there and trying hard to make ends meet.

Elise drove in to Pauillac and turned left off the main road, they passed a supermarket and then found themselves on the Rue Jules Verne. This was it. There was no going back now. Gilbert looked at Elise.

She smiled encouragingly at him, "Deep breaths, Monsieur. He is not a monster."

They got out of the car and crossed the road. 4 Rue Jules Verne was a spacious detached single storey dwelling. What the British would call a bungalow. The house appeared to be in good order. He took a deep breath and knocked on the door.

After a small delay of a few seconds, he could hear the thud of high-heeled shoes as they made their way across bare floorboards to the door. In the glass, he could see the outline of an unmistakable female figure. The door opened. Gilbert nearly fainted or had a heart attack. Standing in the doorway was his mother. He jumped back.

"Jesus Christ. Mum. Fucking Hell. They told me you were dead."

The woman just looked at him with a small smile playing about her lips, "Hello Gilbert. Welcome home."

The woman stepped aside. Standing behind her was an old man of about eighty. He had white hair and a short trimmed white beard. He was the spit and image of Gilbert. He smiled and opened his arms wide, "Hello son. Welcome home."

Gilbert just stared for a few seconds. He could barely move. Something inside him was clicking in to place. Jigsaw pieces were moving across the table at top speed and a picture was emerging. In the end he could only see the smile and the offered embrace. He walked forward in to his father's arms and hugged him tightly, "Hello Dad. Fancy meeting you here."

The old man laughed and turned to look at Elise, "Well, if

it isn't Miss Fancy Pants. I haven't seen you since you were a boy."

Elise burst out laughing, "I got rid of the trousers after you mocked me, and I'm a girl in case you hadn't noticed."

Monsieur Martin looked her up and down, "I can see that, Elise. Come in, both of you. I'll make a pot of coffee."

They walked in to the low-ceilinged hallway and straight on in to the kitchen. Gilbert looked around. There was a fire in the hearth but the units and cooker had all been recently upgraded. It was very nice. They sat down at a polished mahogany table. Gilbert had the feeling that this was all familiar.

The woman spoke first in a distinctly Scottish accent, "I'm not your mother, by the way, I'm your auntie Elizabeth. I take it Margaret's pegged it?"

Gilbert glanced at Elise as if to say "I forgot that one" but he nodded his head, "Yes. She died two days ago, I think. I got a phone call yesterday."

Elizabeth looked at him strangely, "Why aren't you running home to mourn the passing of your beloved mother?" The question was asked sarcastically and Gilbert sensed there was a danger that things could deteriorate very quickly. He decided to be professional and matter of fact.

He cleared his throat, "The truth is, we weren't that close. Margaux and I moved to London to get away from her. I'm obviously sorry that she has passed away but finding Margaux is much more important to me than going to a funeral."

His aunt just looked at him as if he was from another planet, "You are talking about my daughter who is here, in France, in a coma since a car accident thirty-five years ago. I'm not being funny but I'd like a bit of proof that you are not taking the piss, as it were."

The woman was so like his mother, he wanted to reach out and throttle her. Fortunately, there was a flash of brilliant white light and she was there at his side holding his hand.

"Tell her to ask you anything I would know."

Gilbert swallowed his annoyance, "Ask me anything you like that Margaux would definitely know."

He realised at that moment that he despised this woman just like he had hated his own mother. She was a Scottish smart arse and she was the worst of the genre.

Eventually she leaned forward, "Ask her what Bertrand is?"

Margaux sighed, "What a bitch. It is the pink plastic dildo I found in her handbag."

Gilbert looked at Elise and winked, "It is the pink plastic dildo she found in your handbag."

Gilbert's father roared with laughter. Auntie Elizabeth nearly fell off her chair, "Okay, I believe you. Can I speak to Margaux? How is she?"

The woman's demeanour had changed dramatically. Suddenly, she was full of hope.

Margaux looked at Gilbert. Repeat after me and say every word. He nodded.

Gilbert looked at his Aunt, "Margaux says that she is fine and she is leaving with me, you stupid fucking bitch."

XVI

The Old Man

His Aunt just stared at him sadly, "That figures. Apparently, it is just like old times. I think I'll leave now. I know when I am not wanted."

Gilbert looked apologetic, "I'm sorry. Her words, not mine."

She went in to her pocket and lifted out a set of keys and an electronic ID card. She showed them to the old man and laid them on the table. She nodded once, left the kitchen and walked out through the front door.

His father put the coffee pot on the table and sat down beside them, "She and Margaux never really got on. I don't think anybody really got on since the catastrophe."

The old man poured out three coffees and sipped his drink, "I take it you want the whole story from the beginning?"

Gilbert sat back in his seat, "I think I've worked some of it out but it would be great to hear the tale from the very beginning. I want you to know that I really need the truth and that I'm not going to blame you for anything. I get the distinct impression that blame is the thing that has caused this disaster from the very beginning. From my point of view, I'm just glad you're alive and I'm very happy to see you."

His father put his hand on his, "Thank you, son. Trust me, that one single sentence is going to help a lot."

He took another sip of his coffee and cleared his throat, "It all started here in Pauillac, in the summer of 1968. I had just been made the vigneron at Chateau Lafite and my identical twin brother, Gilbert, was doing very well at Chateau Margaux. Together, we were very happy. We had both just turned thirty and life couldn't have been better, apart from one thing. We were both useless with women.

I genuinely believe that most identical twins have problems with the opposite sex, it has something to do with the fact that there is a person in your life who is the same as you, in every way. A prospective wife just can't get over the fact that she might not be the most important person in your life. You have this clone walking about and when they say jump, you jump. When they say run, you run. You have no choice.

Imagine our delight when a pair of identical twins turn up from Scotland for the grape harvest. It seemed absolutely perfect. I fell in love with Margaret and Gilbert fell in love with Elizabeth. It was all so easy. We understood each other. We all knew what it was like to be an identical twin.

In the summer of 1969, we got married here in Pauillac. All four of us lived in this house and we all went on honeymoon to Edinburgh. I met your grandparents and everything was fine. Whilst we were there, we went up north to a place called Royal Dornoch and we stayed in a caravan for a week. We went walking in the hills and even swam in the sea. It was a great summer.

One night, in the caravan, we started drinking wine and we got talking about children. Somehow, we got on to the idea that we could conduct an experiment. We asked the question. If we had a baby at the same time, would the children be twins, siblings, or cousins? It was a silly little thing but the girls loved the idea and they became quite obsessed with it. It wasn't long before we were all having it off in the same bed."

The old man paused and sipped his coffee. He looked around for a reaction and was met with snickering from both

Elise and Gilbert. They both started to tear. Gilbert held his nose in an attempt to stop the outburst but he just couldn't. Pretty soon both he and Elise were in stitches.

The old man chuckled indulgently, "I see all three of you are cut from the same cloth. Margaux was the same as you pair. She always had a wicked sense of humour. The thing is. Doing that sort of thing isn't a big deal for identical twins. Not really. It felt perfectly normal. Anyway, the girls got pregnant at the same time and both you and Margaux heaved in to view on 22 March 1970. Exactly the same day and exactly the same hour. You were born first at twenty past two and Margaux came along at half past. It was astonishing.

The only thing that caused a little bit of disappointment was that you were different sexes but that wasn't a big deal. Certainly not for me. I called my boy Gilbert after my brother and he called his daughter Margaux, after the Chateau where he worked. I think he had it in his head that she would come and work for him when she was older. It was a good idea.

Everything was fine for six months and then disaster. My brother Gilbert had been following a band called Storm. They were a rock group that we had seen in Paris. They were playing a live gig at a nightclub in Saint-Laurent-du-Pont. It is only eight hours away in the car and he persuaded me that it would be a good idea to go for a night out. Everybody was fine about it so we went.

That night was one of the worst fires I can remember. We were both drunk and outside the club when Gilbert said that he needed to go for a piss. I never saw him again. The place went up like a bonfire. 146 people were killed including Gilbert and the band. I couldn't identify the body, they were so badly burned.

When I came home, there was hell to pay. Suddenly the situation had changed. We were no longer a foursome. It was now an awkward twosome and one extra. Elizabeth kept asking me why I hadn't saved my brother. Why did I let him go alone? For fuck's sake, we were close but I didn't go to the bathroom every time he needed a piss.

What really pissed me off was the fact that I had lost my brother and not one person showed me any compassion. I was pretty angry and feeling very stressed. Anyway, I turned to drink in quite a big way."

He paused again and took another sip of his coffee. He was staring out of the window as if reliving the past. Gilbert put his hand on his father's back. The truth was, he really liked his old man and he had a huge amount of compassion for him. He'd lost his brother and it didn't come as any surprise that his mother hadn't helped him.

At last his father came out of his reverie, "One night, after a huge drinking session, I came home. I went to bed with you and your mother. In the middle of the night, I woke up and needed to go for a piss. I went to the bathroom and when I came out, Elizabeth was standing on the landing, naked and crying. I asked her what was wrong and she said that she couldn't bare it any more, she missed Gilbert so much. I gave her a hug. That is all. Unfortunately, at that precise moment your mother walked out and caught us apparently in flagrante.

Your mother went mad and accused us of having an affair behind her back. The following morning, she packed her bags and left for Scotland. That was the last I saw of you. From that point on we corresponded through lawyers. I was barred from seeing you and you were raised a citizen of the United Kingdom when in actual fact you are French.

The truth is, I think your mother was looking for an excuse to leave. She had become tired of my drinking and she had become tired of her sister who did nothing but whine. It was appalling.

Anyway, for the sake of my work, I had to clean myself

up a bit. I left Lafite and moved to Margaux and took up the job that Gilbert was doing there. I then became the vigneron.

I was left with my brother's wife and my brother's daughter. Although, it turned out to be a mistake, I wanted to do the right thing. I didn't want Margaux to grow up without a father so when the divorce came through, I married Elizabeth and adopted Margaux.

And then we come to you. When Margaux was about eleven, she started asking questions. There were rumours flying about and it is very difficult to keep things quiet. Especially here in small villages where everybody knows everybody else's business.

She hated her mother and went around telling her friends that she was her stepmother. This just added fuel to the fire. In the end, I told her the truth to keep her quiet. Another one of my many mistakes. Unbeknownst to me, she was in touch with her Scottish Grandparents.

In the summer of 1983, they told her that you were coming to France. To La Rochelle. Not only that, they told her when you were visiting Châtelaillon-Plage."

Gilbert nodded, "Yes. They made me phone them several times. I wondered what that was all about."

His father nodded, "Well, she managed to persuade her mother to take her there on the day you visited. I think she wanted to leave home and go to Scotland with you."

Gilbert chuckled, "That is exactly what she did do".

His father looked at him, "I know. When she left you on the beach, she can't have been looking where she was going. She walked straight in front of a car and was knocked over. She has been in a coma ever since. The funny thing is, the doctors didn't think there was that much wrong with her. She really should have woken up but she hasn't batted an eyelid in thirty-five years."

Gilbert could barely contain himself, "Where is she now?"

His father looked at him and smiled. It was a beautiful smile, "You'll like this. She is in a nursing home that overlooks Châtelaillon-Plage. She has been there all the time. Waiting for you."

Gilbert felt his eyes watering. In the end he couldn't help it. He burst in to tears.

Immediately the old man put his arms around his son, "It is alright, Gilbert. I can take you there tomorrow."

A small voice at his side whispered in his ear, "No. Wait a day, stay with our father tonight and tomorrow. Give me time to get ready."

Gilbert's voice shook, "She says we have to wait a day. She needs time to prepare."

The old man looked up and around the room, "That's my drama queen, alright."

They all laughed. Even Margaux giggled. She knew very well that she was guilty as charged.

The old man got up from his seat and went to the cooker, "I'd better put the dinner on."

He went to the fridge and pulled out various bits and pieces. There was a lamb's leg, carrots, potatoes, and green beans, "I think I will make a roast leg of lamb with all the trimmings."

He prepared the lamb and put it in to the oven. Elise peeled the potatoes and put them and the carrots in a big pot full of water, ready for boiling. Gilbert cut the green beans and blanched them in boiling water, ready for flash frying.

Suddenly his father jolted upright as if a thought had jumped in to his head, "Oh, I nearly forgot, being in my line of work has certain advantages."

He mysteriously disappeared. Five minutes later he returned carrying three dusty bottles, "I've been saving these for you, my boy. No arguments, I'm going to open all three tonight."

XVIII

The Jolly Swag Man

With trembling hands, Gilbert looked at the labels. The first was a Chateau Margaux 1929, the second, a Chateau Lafite 1945 and the third, a Chateau Haut-Brion 1989. Each one of these bottles had attained a mythical status. He was looking at collective swag that could buy him a new Mercedes if he sold them on the open market. Yet, his father was going to open them for him and they were going to drink them together. He could have cried.

Gilbert could barely speak, "Dad, this is treasure beyond imagining."

His dad turned around and looked at him, "No, son, they are just bottles of wine. I'm looking at treasure beyond imagining."

Margaux put her hand in to his, "That is why I love him so much. I must go now. When I see you again, I hope things will be different". There was the usual flash of white light and she disappeared.

The old man sat down at the table, "So, tell me. What happened to your mother?"

Gilbert made a face, "I think I might have killed her by accident. I had already come to France when Elise showed me a picture of a trip to Le Chapon Fin on her birthday. Obviously, I got a bit of a fright when I saw you in the photograph. Mum told me that you died in the Royal Navy when I was two.

I phoned her that night and she went mad. She kept on referring to the fucking cunts which I now presume to be you and Elizabeth."

His father scratched his chin, "Don't forget that your mother thought that Elizabeth and I were having an affair. She wouldn't necessarily have known that we went on to get married. I think, in her head, she must have convinced herself that I was choosing Margaux over you.

This is, of course, complete nonsense but your mother was quite good at convincing herself of something when it suited her.

My own feeling is that she just didn't want to be married to a drunk and couldn't cope with the awkward situation anymore. When she had made her mind up, that was that.

I cannot tell you the pain that she has caused. Over the years, I have spent many regretful moments blaming myself over the business with Elizabeth but the cold hard fact is, nothing happened. That one incident destroyed things for Elizabeth too. She was never able to return home to Scotland. She never saw her parents again before they died and poor Margaux only knew her grandparents by long distance phone call. It was a complete disaster."

The old man looked directly at Gilbert, "Thank you for not blaming me. You missed out on having a father around. It can't have been easy, living with your mother."

Gilbert nodded, "Margaux and I used to call her the cold fish. She was not the loving or hugging type. If I hadn't had Margaux, God knows what I would have done."

The old man propped his arm on the table and laid his cheek in his hand, "Tell me what happened with Margaux. How did you meet?"

Gilbert related the tale of the meeting on Châtelaillon-Plage and the subsequent meeting at the hotel, "At first, I thought I was imagining things but then I realised it was for real. I think that she was determined to come home with me and that is exactly what she did."

His father pondered things for a few moments. In the end, he sighed, "I'm not surprised. You've seen what her mother is like. She made the poor girl's life a misery. Both Margaret and Elizabeth were cut from the same cloth. Gilbert's death merely exposed their natural hideousness. I wish I had seen it sooner but that is now water under the bridge."

Gilbert put his hand on the table, "Listen Dad. I believe you. There is no point in blaming yourself or anyone else for that matter. Mum is dead. She can't hurt us now and you are now divorced from Elizabeth. Draw a line under things and move on. I hereby order you to exorcise the ghosts. No more blaming. No more unhappiness."

His old man smiled, "You were correctly named Gilbert. You are exactly like him in every way."

They sat talking about various things for hours while the lamb roasted in the oven. The old man decanted the Chateau Margaux 1929 and place the decanter on a dresser in the kitchen, "It is the perfect place to bring the wine to the correct temperature."

Gilbert chuckled, "It's funny. Margaux and I were talking about that very vintage before we left London. I told her that I would try and find a bottle when I was in France."

The old man looked pleased, "It was your heritage calling you. You are from a very long line of Medoc vintners. You can trace your family tree back to Jacques de Ségur. He was born in the seventeenth century and planted the vineyards at Chateau Lafite."

Gilbert was stunned, "Is that true?"

His father laughed, "You're damned right it's true. You are a winemaker of the Medoc. It is in your blood."

Elise looked delighted. She walked across the kitchen and pulled Gilbert in to an embrace, "I told you, Monsieur. I said exactly that. It is in your blood."

When dinner was served, the day outside was descending in to twilight. It created an orange glow in the kitchen. The mahogany table looked perfect.

Monsieur Martin, the old vigneron of the great estates of the Medoc picked up the decanter and poured his son a glass of the Chateau Margaux 1929, "Now. I would like to hear your thoughts."

Gilbert picked up the glass and took a sip. He closed his eyes and let the bright red liquid linger on his palette before swallowing. He savoured the moment and let his jumbled thoughts fall in to place before he cleared his throat.

"Old library and cigar boxes with the faint hint of tobacco. Cherry blossoms, sweet soft spices, and red berries. Faint hint of vinegar at the end. The wine is melancholy in a good way. It reminds one of not only what once was but encourages one to think of what could be. It is both regretful and hopeful at the same time. It perfectly sums up our situation."

His father raised his eyebrows and took a sip himself, "Definite hint of cherry and tobacco. I see what you mean about the old library. There are two schools of thought on this. On the one hand you could argue that the wine is a little bit past its prime but on the other you could laud it as a taste of living history. This is the great depression in a glass. Melancholy is a good word to describe it."

They both looked at Elise. She swirled the liquid around in her glass and raised it to her nose, "Definite bouquet of cherry blossom". She took a sip and held the wine in her mouth for a few seconds before swallowing, "Exquisite texture, thin at the end. I detect sweet cherries and red berries. Hint of spice and a slight sourness on the finish. My feeling is that, had we drunk this twenty years ago, it would have been a perfect experience. Even now, it is still astonishing. I'd give it 98 out of 100."

Gilbert nodded, "I think you are right 98 out of 100."

The old man looked impressed, "I can see that you both are the people you were born to be. I give it 95 out of 100 but then again, I am a perfectionist. I think you are right about the twenty years. This would have been perfect at the turn of the millennium and I remember being very tempted to open it then." He looked at Gilbert, "I'm glad I didn't."

The lamb was out of this world. It was succulent and had been cooked à point. Just how Gilbert liked it. When the meal was finished, his father decanted the Lafite '45, "We'll give this an hour and, in the meantime, we can enjoy a little bit of cheese."

They finished the Margaux with the cheeseboard. Gilbert was lingering over a piece of reblochon when he remembered about something he'd been meaning to ask, "Do you still have the old Citroen?"

His father looked utterly astonished, "How do you know about that?"

Gilbert chuckled, "It was one of the few things that Margaux remembered. She always talked about the car. I think she was very fond of it."

The old man smiled, "Yes, now that I remember, she did like the car. The funny thing is, it was never mine. It belonged to her father, Gilbert. When Elizabeth and I divorced, the old car went with her, as was right."

Gilbert was disappointed. He remembered the conversation he had had with Eleanor, "Did the car have a name, by any chance?"

His father looked at him oddly, "What do you mean? It was called a DS which comes from Déesse or Goddess in French. Margaux called it la merde métallique on account of the brown colour."

They all laughed. So much for that romantic notion, thought Gilbert.

When it came time to pour the Lafite '45. Gilbert started shaking with anticipation, "It looks a great colour."

The old man chuckled, "Your Grandfather would be pleased. This is his vintage. He joined Lafite when he was 18, in 1933. During the war, we were part of the occupied zone on account of our proximity to the coast.

When the allies invaded Normandy in 1944, all the signs were there that the following year was going to be a great vintage. It was almost as if the fates conspired to make it happen. Out with the Nazi's and to celebrate, in with the great vintage of the century. It is funny how these things work out."

The old man poured three glasses. This time it was the turn of Elise to go first. She swirled the liquid in her glass and lifted it to her nose, "Definite bouquet of crème de cassis." She took a good sip, "Rosewood, herbs and slight hint of Parma violet. Exquisite and complex. I like this. It is the best wine I have ever tasted."

The smile that Monsieur Martin flashed her spoke volumes.

Gilbert gingerly took a sip, "I detect the blackcurrant and wood. I also think I taste just a hint of crème de menthe. It is definitely complex. I predict that this will get better as we go down the bottle."

The old man laughed delightedly, "I think I'm going to employ both of you. Well done, I have nothing further to add. You have said it all."

Gilbert was dying to ask his next question, "How much have you saved over the years?"

The twinkle on the old man's eye was a picture, "Follow me."

They walked to the end of the kitchen and in to the hall. About halfway along the corridor was a half- opened door. He turned on the light and stepped on to a very tight staircase, "Watch your step", he warned.

They went down twelve steps and entered a cellar that was just as big as the kitchen above their heads. It was packed to the rafters.

Gilbert stood with his mouth open, "Oh my God. It is Aladdin's cave."

Elise was equally impressed, "Mon Dieu, Monsieur. It is the wealth of nations."

Gilbert calculated that there were at least 800 bottles of wine.

His father walked along the shelving holding out his arm, "Your great-grandfather, your grandfather, your uncle, me. This is the collection of three generations. Every single one a classic in its own way. It is yours now, son. Yours and Margaux's. It is the inheritance of Medoc and Bordeaux."

XVIII

The Window in the Corner

Gilbert was speechless. He started walking along the shelves. There were wines from Pauillac, St Estephe, St Julien, Margaux, Sauternes, Pessac-Leognan, Pomerol and St Emillion.

His head was in a spin. Lafite, Latour, Mouton, d'Yquem, Leoville, Haut-Brion, Petrus, Cheval-Blanc, and Margaux. 1899, 1921, 1928, 1929, 1945, 1959 and the modern vintages were there in abundance. There were 6 bottles of the 1989 Petrus. A whole section was dedicated to the 2009 vintage from all the great vineyards.

Gilbert could barely breathe, "Good heavens, Dad. I think I'm going to faint."

His father laughed. Pick a good one for Sunday. It is Easter and the day we go to see Margaux. Make it one she will remember."

Gilbert knew exactly which one to pick. He lifted one of the 1989 Petrus from its rack, "Surely, this is the pick of the bunch."

His father nodded, "You don't disappoint. Yes, I agree. That is the one we will have on Sunday."

Gilbert held the bottle tightly to his body as they all made their way back to the kitchen.

His father went to the kettle, "Time for a cup of coffee."

They sat for hours at the mahogany table, sipping wine and drinking coffee. At the end of the evening, when it was time for bed, his father turned to Gilbert, "There is something I must do, tomorrow, before we go to see Margaux on Sunday. Will you be alright here, on your own?"

Gilbert thought about it for a moment and then looked at Elise, "If you are going to be away, Elise and I could return to our hotel in La Rochelle and get our things. We could stay there tomorrow night and then meet you at Châtelaillon-Plage."

His father nodded, "That is a good idea. Let me give you the address." He wrote a note and handed it to Gilbert.

Maison de Repos St Martin
Châtelaillon-Plage

Gilbert smiled, "I think I know why you chose this place."

The old man smiled, "Yes. It is obvious. Having said that, everything about the place was perfect. Her room has a single corner window which looks down the length of the beach. It felt right."

When it was time for bed, the old man took them upstairs and showed them to their bedrooms. He hugged his father and said goodnight. He went in to his room and removed his trousers and shirt and climbed in to the single bed. He was asleep before his head hit the pillow.

When he awoke in the morning. His father had gone. There was a note on the kitchen table asking them to help themselves to breakfast. They made coffee and toast and sat at the table. Gilbert took a sip of his coffee, "Shall we just head straight back up to La Rochelle?" Elise bit in to a slice of toast, "Can you give me an hour or two? I'd like to drop in on my parents whilst I am here. We have plenty of time."

Gilbert nodded, "Of course. What time do you want to come back here?"

She looked at him speculatively, "Two o'clock? That way,

we'll be back at the hotel before it starts to get dark."

Gilbert smiled, "Fine. I'll stay here and have a look around. I think I might have another look at the cellar."

Elise chuckled, "Don't smash anything, for God's sake."

He grinned, "Not bloody likely."

Elise finished her breakfast and left. Gilbert washed the dishes and went out in to the hall. The cellar door was closed and he tried the handle. The old man had locked it since last night. Gilbert nearly laughed out loud. He knew him too well, already. He turned around and saw another door facing him. The living room he surmised. He opened the door.

The room was quite small but very well appointed. There was an old traditional fireplace and two leather couches. Gilbert felt an uneasy thrill. His father's tastes were exactly the same as his own.

On the near wall was a dresser and it was filled with photographs. There was the one of himself as a baby being lifted up by his father. It was the same one that his mother had shown him. There were several of Margaux as a young girl with her mother. Gilbert was struck again by the exact likeness between his own mother and his aunt.

When he got to the end of the dresser, there was one of Margaux on the beach in her shorts standing in front of a group of people. He looked closely at the photograph. Suddenly, the hairs on the back of his neck started to rise. She was wearing the same outfit that he had painted her in the picture that had won the Trinity prize. It was Margaux on the day he had met her on Châtelaillon-Plage. He was certain of it.

He looked at the people sitting on a blanket, behind her on the sand. That dreadful feeling came over him again. His skin felt clammy and a chill coursed through his body. He had to sit down. It didn't make any sense.

He calmed himself and stood up again. He picked up the

photograph and looked at it closely once more. There was no mistake. He was absolutely certain. Sitting on the blanket were his aunt, his father, the woman from Le Chapon Fin and none other than Elise Simon. There was no mistake. His father, Elise and her mother were on Châtelaillon-Plage on the day Margaux had her accident.

Gilbert breathed out, "Fucking hell. What the fuck is going on?"

There was a familiar flash of brilliant white light and she was there at his side. She looked up at him and she was so sad. Gilbert looked in to her eyes and experienced a moment of supernatural insight. The girl who was standing before him had arranged everything in order so that he could be brought to this point, at this time.

He was so utterly certain of that, he was able to make a decision right there and then. He loved this girl so much that he would do anything she needed him to do. It didn't matter to him. His own heart was standing in front of him. He smiled.

"We are both the same, Madame. What do you need me to do?"

She smiled at him and it was a smile that was full of love, "I need you to forgive."

He bent down and picked her up, "I will do anything you need me to do. I will forgive any sin. Just tell me what you want me to know. I will draw a line under it. I will move on. I will do all of these things on your behalf. Tell me."

She kissed him and laid her head on his shoulder, "You have worked out by now that it was no accident that I arrived on Châtelaillon-Plage that day. Your father and I have been in this since the very beginning. He was desperate to see his son and I longed to meet my twin.

Everything went like clockwork until the last minute. After I handed you the letter, I turned around so that I could get a final glimpse of you. I waved as you got on the coach. I wasn't looking where I was going. I stepped on to the road and was hit by a car. It was a brown Citroen DS. My father's car driven by your father.

The accident nearly killed him. So much bad luck. So much pain. He needs you to let him get over it. It was not his fault. You stand at a Quatre-bras. If you go one way, you will destroy everything, like our mothers have tried to destroy everything in their lust for vengeance and blame or you could go the other way and bring everybody back from the dead.

Who are you, Gilbert? Are you our mothers or are you our fathers?"

He looked at her, "Who are you, Madame?"

She smiled, "I am our fathers. Winemakers from the Medoc. The fruit of the vine."

He kissed her, "We are both the same, Madame. We always have been. I will bring everyone back from the dead."

She hugged him fiercely, "Put the photograph back on the dresser and play out my game. In a room with a window in the corner, I am waiting for you."

He put the photograph back where it belonged, "I've been moving through the silence without motion, waiting for you."

She laughed, "It is truly, uncanny how we are wired together."

He chuckled, "We have all of eternity to look forward to. I am coming for you. Nothing can stop that now."

She held her fingers to her lips, "Say nothing. There is no point. Let them have their day. Let them have their victory."

He nodded, "Whatever you say, my love. Where has my father gone today?"

She laughed, "He has gone to buy me a new dress, of course. What else could be so important?"

He laughed in return. There was a flash of light and Gilbert was alone once again, but not for long.

At two o'clock, he was already waiting outside the house. Elise pulled up in the car and he jumped in.

She looked at him, "La Rochelle?"

He smiled, "I think that would be a very good idea."

Elise took the road north towards the Pointe de Grave, "I think it would be nice to take the ferry."

Gilbert happily agreed. He felt he could agree to anything at this point. He was happier now than he had ever been. He felt as if his soul had been cleansed.

He thought about how Margaux had manipulated him in to this beautiful position of hope and renewal at Easter. Nothing had been left to chance. The regrets of Elise, the warnings from Monsieur Delmas and all the perfectly timed e-mails from Eleanor pushing him in the right direction at the right moment.

He chuckled to himself. He wondered how many people were involved. Knowing Margaux, probably a cast of thousands.

Elise looked at him, "Why are you so happy?"

He laughed, "I had a visit from our mutual friend. Everything is ready. All we have to do is turn up tomorrow."

Elise said nothing. She looked like a cat who had just found a mouse overdosing on cream. Her face was a picture.

They crossed the Gironde estuary in glorious sunshine. Halfway, there was a light shower. Just enough to create the most wonderful rainbow over the Bay of Biscay. It was perfect.

At Rayon, they took the road north to Rochefort and then on to La Rochelle. They arrived at their hotel at four-thirty.

Gilbert looked at Elise, "I think I'm going to take a nap for the rest of the afternoon. I can meet you for dinner at say, seven-thirty?"

She nodded, "Good idea. I'm a little bit tired, myself.

Seven-thirty will be perfect."

When Gilbert got back to his room, he couldn't sleep. He was too excited. He decided to lay out everything in preparation for tomorrow. He looked out his best black suit. It had been handmade in Savile Row and had cost him a fortune. He wiped his black leather shoes. And laid out his best blue tie. He had bought it at the Palais de Versailles and had little golden fleur de lys woven through it.

Finally, he looked out his black soft leather rucksack and placed the item he had bought in Pessac, carefully at the bottom. He zipped it up. He looked at what he had laid out. He was happy. He was ready.

He dined with Elise and drank just enough wine to make him sleepy. When he returned to his room, he was definitely tired. He changed in to his pyjamas and slipped under the covers.

XIX

Hallelujah, In Ewigkeit

When Gilbert awoke in the morning, he got out of bed and showered carefully. He scrubbed away all the accumulated dirt of the last few days and ensured he was as clean as he possibly could be. He shaved and applied the Boucheron that Margaux had bought for him.

He dressed in to his fine black suit, a white shirt, his blue tie and his black leather shoes. When he looked in the mirror, it was clear that he had taken care over his appearance. He picked up his leather rucksack and opened the door.

Elise was waiting on the landing. She, too, had taken great care. She looked appropriately expensive. He smiled at her, "Breakfast?"

She nodded, "Yes. Let's have a cup of coffee. I think I need it to calm my nerves."

He knew what she meant. He was very nervous, too.

At breakfast, he had a plate of fruit and some toast with marmalade. The cup of coffee was just what he needed to settle himself down a bit. He looked over the table at Elise. She was wearing a small golden cross with a sunburst at the centre. He lifted his finger and pointed to it, "Very apt choice, if you don't mind me saying."

She smiled, "Let's hope so. It is Easter Sunday, after all."

At 9.30, they jumped in the car. They fastened their seat belts and Elise started the engine, "Here we go". She put her foot on the throttle and they were off to Châtelaillon-Plage.

The morning was golden and glorious. The sun seemed to infuse everything they looked at with a pale-yellow glow. In the car park, his father was already waiting for them. He looked as if he was also in his best suit.

He waved as they approached, "I hope you have had a nice morning."

Gilbert hugged him, "We've been a bit nervous but we have managed a decent breakfast."

He looked at both of them, "Are you ready?"

Gilbert nodded, "Yes. I'm as ready as I'll ever be."

The old man's face assumed a determined look, "Then, let's go."

He walked them to the door of the nursing home and opened it with his key. Once inside, they climbed a flight of stairs and walked along the corridor to the end.

In front of them was a door. His father pulled out an electronic swipe card and waved it in front of a black electronic reader. There was a click and the door opened a fraction. He turned around and looked at them both. He smiled and nodded. This was it. No going back now.

When they went inside, a bed was situated directly in front of them. It was bathed in sunlight from a huge bay window in the corner of the room. Gilbert looked out of the window and could see the whole length of the beach. It looked just as he remembered it. Golden-red and ochre. The sea was a magnificent shade of turquoise.

Gilbert could hear the slow methodical breathing of someone who is on life support. He looked at the body in the bed. There was no doubt. This was Margaux Martin, whom he had met on this very beach, thirty-five years ago. She was older, more beautiful but it was definitely his cousin-twin.

She lay on the top of the quilt. It was obvious to Gilbert that her hair had been done and she was wearing the new dress his father had bought for her. She looked happy and at peace.

At the side of the bed, sitting on a chair, was his aunt, "I hope you don't mind me being here. I don't want to intrude or anything."

Gilbert couldn't care less where this woman was at any given moment. The sentence had been said in that smart arse sarcastic fashion that he had known so well over the years. He sighed. He was about to say something when his father interjected.

"Shut the fuck up, Elizabeth. Nobody is in any mood for your twisted commentary, today. Stay, if you like but keep quiet. If you can't manage that then I suggest you fuck off."

His aunt Elizabeth shrank back in her chair. She had the look of the coward who suddenly realises that they've gone too far. She would not be allowed to spoil the moment. Gilbert smiled. Well said Dad, he thought. As he stood at the end of the bed, he suddenly realised that he didn't know what to do.

A small voice whispered in his ear, "Don't worry. You have done all that you needed to do. You are here. You have brought me home. Don't you understand? I have been in your head all this time. We are the same, Monsieur. I can live in me and I can live in you. Nobody else. Just you."

Gilbert let his mouth drop open. It made perfect sense to him, now. They were both the same. The little girl who had followed him off the beach all those years ago, had somehow jumped in to his head. He didn't understand how it was possible but he understood it. It made perfect sense. They were both the same.

He felt it before he heard it. It started with a small vibration and gathered pace. After about thirty seconds, the vibration became a hum and then the hum seemed to expand and become voices. It was like the sound of a choir that started slowly, only to build up to a huge crescendo.

Gilbert smiled. It reminded him of a piece of music that

he and Margaux loved and were very familiar with. The sound reminded him of the pilgrim's chorus from Wagner's Tannhäuser.

He played the music in his head. As the song progressed, the light in the room got brighter. His drama queen had decided to make an entrance. He laughed out loud.

Through penance and repentance, I have propitiated
The Lord, Whom my heart serves,
Who crowns my repentance with blessing,
The Lord to Whom my song goes up!

The salvation of pardon is granted the penitent,
In days to come He will walk in the peace of the blessed!

Hell and death do not appal Him,
Therefore, will I praise God my life long.

Alleluia! Alleluia in eternity
Hallelujah! Hallelujah! In Ewigkeit!

There was a flash of white light and he felt her leave him. The body on the bed twitched. Gilbert heard a rushing sound. Margaux Martin opened her eyes and sat up.

She looked for one person in the room. The one whom she had just left. He walked round the bed and enfolded her in an embrace. He pulled her head back and kissed her on the mouth. Then again and again and again.

When she started to laugh, he let her go and knelt down.

He went in to his rucksack and pulled out the gift he had bought for her in Pessac. He put it in his right hand and held it out for her. It was a chocolate egg wrapped in gold. It looked hideously expensive.

Margaux looked at the gift and laughed, "We are definitely both the same. The question I have for you is this. Did you buy it or did I?"

He laughed. He didn't care, "I think I've worked out where my special powers came from. I know fine well that you made me buy it. I also know that you bought it to share it."

It was her turn to laugh out loud, "We'll see about that!"

Gilbert stepped back from the bed to let the others in. Her mother came forward first. Her face was awed. Somehow, she had changed a little bit. Some of the anger and vitriol had disappeared. She was happy to see her daughter, "Welcome back, darling."

Margaux smiled at her and pulled her in to a fierce embrace. Her mother burst in to tears.

That's one brought back from the dead, thought Gilbert.

His father moved forward and she pulled him in to the same tight hug. He, too, could not contain himself. Tears fell to his cheeks.

That's two.

Finally, Elise rushed forward and was given the same treatment.

Three.

Margaux looked at all four of them, "Well, here we all are. Before you start giving me advice about being careful, I will remind you that I have been cooped for thirty-five years, so if you don't mind…"

She shuffled her bottom to the side of the bed and held her arm out for Gilbert. He stepped forward and helped her up. Her legs were weak.

She leaned on him, "Legs are a bit weak but all things considered. Not too bad. Better than I expected."

Gilbert walked her about the room for a minute or two and then she sat on the bed again.

She rubbed her thighs, "Give me a minute or two and I'll be fine."

At that point in time, not one of them had the audacity to give her any advice at all. They let her do her own thing. After a minute she turned to her mother, "Did you bring the merde métallique with you?"

Her mother burst out laughing, "Of course. It's the only car I've ever had."

Margaux nodded happily, "When I am ready. We are all going for a lavish Easter Sunday lunch. I have booked us in to Cristopher Coutanceau. Don't worry. Gilbert is paying."

He nodded happily, "Yes. I'm paying. I hope they have a very good wine list."

She chuckled, "Would I ever let you down."

When she was ready, Margaux put her arms around Gilbert and his father. Together, they propped her up as she walked to the door. At the end of the corridor, they took the lift instead of the stairs.

In the car park, they walked past the Audi and on to the Citroen DS. Gilbert wondered how he had missed it. It gleamed in the sunshine.

Elizabeth opened the passenger door and turned around, "I've just had her done up. She's as good as new."

Margaux smiled at her, "I wonder what made you decide to do that?"

Her mother shrugged, "I don't know. It just came to me in a flash."

They all burst out laughing. They put Margaux in the back seat, between Elise and Gilbert. Elizabeth got behind the wheel and Gilbert's father jumped in to the passenger seat.

Her mother looked in the rear-view mirror, "Where is this restaurant?"

Margaux leaned forward, "It is on the Quayside, just beyond the tour de la Lanterne."

Elizabeth started the car and they were on their way. Twenty minutes later, they pulled up at the restaurant. It looked very modern and geometrical. There was a flight of stairs leading up to the restaurant floor.

Margaux spied the steps, "Don't worry about the climb. It will be worth it for the view."

In the end, Gilbert and his father just lifted her up the steps without her having to trouble with anything at all. They walked in and approached the maître.

Margaux smiled, "Table pour cinq, s'il vous plait. Au nom de Martin."

The waiter showed them to a large table in front of the window which overlooked the Bay of Biscay. It was perfect.

They sat round the table and picked up their menus. It wasn't long before Gilbert was chuckling.

Margaux elbowed him in the ribs, "What's so funny?"

He scratched his chin, "By some divine co-incidence. All my favourite dishes appear to be on the menu. Not just one of them but all of them. I wonder how that could have happened?"

She shrugged, "Special powers, I think."

He turned to look at her, "Are you trying to tell me that you are some sort of superhero, Madame?"

She smiled deprecatingly, "Why, Monsieur, that is exactly what I am trying to tell you. I thought you might have worked it out yourself."

XX

Crépuscule

Gilbert addressed the group, "First things first. As today is a special day. When we are honouring not one, but many people coming back from the dead, I think we should celebrate with Champagne."

Margaux tapped the table, "Hear, hear."

He turned to her, "I leave it to you, Madame, to select the best one."

She didn't even need to look at the wine list, "Let's have a bottle of the 2000 Krug."

Gilbert nodded, "Excellent choice, Madame."

They ordered the champagne. When it came, Margaux popped the bottle and poured out five glasses. Gilbert was delighted to see that they were the flat-bottomed champagne glasses and not the flutes.

He lifted his glass, "To forgiveness, to resurrection and to Margaux Martin."

Margaux looked at him out of the corner of her eye, "Are you drunk already, Monsieur?"

They all fell about laughing.

The meal was sumptuous. They ordered every dish from the starter tasting menu and helped themselves. There were oysters, moules, langoustines in garlic butter, grenouille and every other dish that Gilbert had ever taken a liking to.

Gilbert looked at Margaux, "Madame, you would think you hadn't eaten in thirty-five years."

She couldn't care less, "I'm making up for it, Monsieur. It is all very well eating through someone else but tasting it, in your own mouth, makes a big difference."

He was suddenly curious, "What was it like?"

She smiled at him, "It was wonderful. Don't worry about that. I felt everything that you felt, I knew everything that you thought. I'm very interested to know if I still have the capabilities. I'm getting the distinct impression that I do."

He sat back in his seat, "What am I thinking?" he thought of something obscure.

She didn't stop eating, "You are thinking of our painting, now hanging in the Royal Academy."

Gilbert jumped. She was correct.

She looked at him as if he was a dolt, "What am I thinking?"

Suddenly, the image of a bottle of Chateau Margaux popped in to his mind, "You are thinking of the Chateau Margaux 1983."

She chuckled, "Yes please, it will go well with the beef dish I have ordered for the main course."

Gilbert burst out laughing and ordered the wine. This meal was definitely going to cost him a fortune but he didn't mind. The money he was making from the sale of his book was as much Margaux's as it was his. She probably wrote half of it anyway.

She giggled, "A bit more than half, I think."

He immediately had a thought, "Who were the ones who were calling you."

She shrugged, "I think you know the answer to that question already. It was my father and my grandparents. Lots of them. They were making plans in case things didn't work out. In the end, it was unnecessary. Here I am, after all."

Gilbert looked out of the window. It was still lunchtime but the sun had started to take on that orange hue. It would become golden red before long and the Bay of Biscay would transition from that bright turquoise blue to the green shade of late afternoon.

She put her hand on his, "Normally, at this point, people say are you thinking what I'm thinking but I don't think that is necessary today. You are thinking what I'm thinking. It will be alright. Don't worry."

When the main course of beef arrived, Margaux poured out the '83. She lifted it to her lips, "Well, it has been a long time coming, but here goes". She took a surprisingly large mouthful.

Gilbert waited, "Well?"

She savoured every ounce of it, "Cassis, raspberry and a hint of vanilla. The earth on the finish."

The old man sat in his seat chuckling, "I see I have another recruit."

Elise was looking at them speculatively, "What are you going to do now? Where are you going to live?"

Gilbert hadn't really thought that far ahead but Margaux seemed to have made firm plans.

"We are going back to the UK to sell everything. We will sell the house in Edinburgh and the house in Kensington and then we are buying an apartment in Paris and a house near Pauillac. Gilbert is choosing the apartment in Paris and I will take care of the house in the Medoc."

Gilbert nodded. Without realising it, that was exactly what he wanted to do.

Elise looked pleased, "Where in Paris are you thinking."

He grinned, "I've told you already. Haussmann. However, if the prices aren't to my satisfaction then we could choose somewhere nearer the Arc de Triomphe."

She laughed, "Don't worry. I think you will be able to afford it."

They tucked in to the roast beef. Gilbert thought it was

excellent, "I wonder why we don't see this more often in France." He had asked the question, knowing full well the answer.

Elizabeth piped up, "It isn't very French. They associate it with everything British."

There was silence for a moment until everyone started to titter. Gilbert tried not to laugh out loud but, in the end, he couldn't help it. He started roaring. Soon everyone was belly laughing. Even Elizabeth.

Dessert was a chocolate gateau with ice cream. Margaux looked apologetic, "I was hoping to find somewhere that sold your glace malaga."

Gilbert didn't mind. He was happy. In fact, he couldn't remember a happier meal.

When the dessert was over, they ordered coffees and sat round finishing the Margaux.

His father broached the subject he was dreading, "You'll have to go home for the funeral now."

Gilbert nodded, "Yes. I can't delay it any longer. I was thinking that I might as well see to everything whilst I'm there. That way, when I return, I'm here for good."

Margaux picked up her coffee cup, "I'm coming with you."

Gilbert sat silently. He had no intention of letting her out of his sight but he knew he would have to let the others make their objections.

His father cleared his throat, "Are you sure that's wise."

She nodded, "I'm sure. I feel fine. I feel a little weak but that is all. Listen, I know you think this is very strange but I have it on the very best authority that everything will be okay. All these years, someone has been looking out for me. I will be fine."

Gilbert put his hand on hers to show that he would do anything she said.

His father appeared to have come to decision, "Then I'm coming with you. I should really go anyway. She was my wife."

Elizabeth looked at him sadly, "She was my twin sister. I should really come too. Just to be on the safe side."

His father looked at her, "Let's be frank. I'm fine with you coming as long as the right person turns up. If it is the good Elizabeth, then fine. If it is the smart arse, then I stand by what I said earlier. You can fuck off. I can assure you, I'm not going to let you spoil another day of my life. Are we clear?"

Elizabeth looked close to tears. She bowed her head and nodded, "I hear you. I will keep quiet."

Gilbert thought about things for a minute, "Let's settle the plan. Why don't we leave here and return to Châtelaillon-Plage to pick up the Audi? We can head back to Pauillac for a few days to give Margaux a chance to recover. I will book flights for us all to go to Edinburgh from Bordeaux.

We go to Mum's funeral. We head back down to London. I pick up a few must haves from the house and then we return to Pauillac. I can then arrange to do everything from there at leisure. There will be no pressure."

Margaux squeezed his hand, "Sounds like a plan."

His father relaxed, "I'm in."

Elise shrugged, "I have two weeks off work. I can manage that. I'm in."

Elizabeth looked at her daughter, "I'm in." She looked at her husband, "And yes, I'll keep my trap shut."

They all chuckled. Gilbert finished his coffee, "Seems like we have a plan."

Gilbert called for the bill. When it came, he didn't even bat an eyelid. He had paid for more expensive lunches but not by much. It was a fabulous price but then again, it was two-star Michelin restaurant.

Gilbert and his father carried Margaux down the steps to the car. They carefully manoeuvred Margaux in to the middle of the back seat. Gilbert then squeezed in beside her.

Elizabeth turned around and looked at them, "Do you need anything from your hotel?"

Gilbert shook his head, "It's all in the Audi. We checked out this morning."

As they made their way through La Rochelle, Gilbert kept looking at the sky. It was now descending in to the red orange glow that he loved so much. He thought about his painting and cursed himself that he hadn't brought a camera.

When they reached Châtelaillon-Plage, Gilbert realised that his timing, as usual, was perfect.

When they got out of the car, Margaux turned to the others, "I'm afraid, you are going to have to amuse yourselves for a little while. Gilbert and I have one last thing to do before we head back down to Medoc."

The others smiled. They had guessed already that there would be a small delay.

She looked at Gilbert and kissed him. She then put her arm over his shoulder and together they walked down to the beach.

The scene was glorious. The beach was almost empty. As the afternoon sun had started to disappear the sun worshippers had begun to feel the cold and had headed back to their cars.

The sand was the colour of French ochre and the sea was the colour of deep turquoise green. These are the type of colours that make you weep thought Gilbert. No sooner had he thought that then he felt Margaux's free hand grab his free hand. She knew exactly what he was thinking.

At just the right moment he walked in to the bright white surf, "This is where I took my shoes off."

They walked on for a few yards when Margaux stopped,

"This is where I asked if you were English. I didn't really understand the nuances between English and Scottish."

He laughed, "Yes. This is where I said I'm Scottish actually. I'm from Edinburgh. Little did I know I wasn't from Edinburgh at all. I was born in Pauillac."

After a few more yards, Margaux pointed at the sand, "That is where I asked you if you wanted an ice cream."

He chuckled, "Une glace malaga, s'il vous plaît."

She squeezed him, "Your french was good. Even then."

They passed the place where the ice cream vendor was. There was a van selling galletes. Gilbert looked at the sand, "This is where you drew a map of Western Europe and asked me to tell you where the monster lived."

They walked all the way along to the little pools. They sat down on the raised stone. He laid his head on her shoulder, "I love you. I love you with all my heart. I hope your life hasn't been terrible."

She leaned in to him, "My life has been wonderful. I have lived in your head for half a lifetime and been given the opportunity to really feel what it's like to be another person. I know, now, that we are all the same. We have the same feelings, we feel the same pain, we experience the same unfairness, we tolerate the same prejudices, we experience the same sadness.

At the end of the day, there is still love. I am lucky to have had you. I know that you love me more than anything. That is why I developed my super powers so that I could bring you back here on Easter Sunday. In the twilight. On Châtelaillon-Plage."

Index

I	7
The Dorchester Hotel	
II	15
The Dream	
III	22
Margaux	
IV	29
The Royal Academy	
V	36
Châtelaillon-Plage	
VI	43
Bon Anniversaire	
VII	50
The Twitterati	
VIII	57
Paris	
IX	64
Elise Simon	
X	71
Interviews et enquêtes	
XI	78
Zone Interdite	

XII	85
La Rochelle	
XIII	92
Disaster & Dreams	
XIV	99
Médoc	
XV	106
Place de Naissance	
XVI	113
The Old Man	
XVIII	119
The Jolly Swag Man	
XVIII	126
The Window in the Corner	
XIX	133
Hallelujah, In Ewigkeit	
XX	140
Crépuscule	

Finito di stampare nel mese di luglio 2020
presso Rotomail Italia S.p.A. - Vignate (MI)